COLD LAKE ANTHOLOGY

2022

COLD LAKE ANTHOLOGY 2022

SELECTIONS FROM BURLINGTON WRITERS WORKSHOP

Edited by Elaine Pentaleri, Nancy Volkers, Jocelyn Royalty, and Matthew Blanchet

Cold Lake Publishing

First Printing, 2022

Cover art: Susan Smereka

Contents

From the Editors

"Longing, it may be, is the gift no other gift supplies."

-*Emily Dickinson*

None of us is a stranger to yearning, to the ache of longing.

How can we capture the elusive, regain what has been lost, appease our yearnings? The poems and stories featured in this anthology pull at the threads of longing: longing for love, longing for the past, longing for change. Ironically, deep yearnings fill us, compelling us forward and bringing clarity to our intention.

In our opening story, *In the Night Church*, Mark Hoffman leads us through a circuitous past, through interwoven decades and lives, replete with the yearnings of youth and maturity, with an equal measure of nostalgia and hope. In our closing story, *Randy LaRose's Life of Crime*, Masha Harris reveals the yearnings of a young man, yearnings stymied by circumstance, misfortune, and impending ennui. All of the poems and stories featured here present characters at various crossroads, and uncover distinct aspects of longing and fateful responses to it.

We hope you enjoy this year's anthology, and celebrate the writers whose work is featured here.

The Editors
Cold Lake Anthology

In The Night Church

Mark Hoffman

A few days after his mother's funeral, Jake was sitting in one of the wooden pews. The church smelled old, just as it had many years ago, when they'd brought him here on Sundays. The smell hadn't changed, and the space seemed much as he remembered; half in shadow now, since the stained-glass windows were muted by the dark, but some were lit from the outside, and the fixtures in the small church made the half-light very comfortable. His son was with cousins for dinner, probably playing some board game now, Nathaniel laughing and chatting after the meal. Jake had met with an old friend downtown, sharing the nostalgia just as they shared the familiar entrees between them, until it was time for a hug and one last smile, time to rejoin their separate lives again. He'd stopped here in the entryway for some warmth on his way to the car, then gone inside to sit among these memories for a moment. It had been a week of sharing memories, and tomorrow the two of them would make the long drive back home.

Jake looked around the open space. Oak, carved ornament, and stained glass were still the main features here; all the wood probably accounted for that familiar smell, like the old houses he'd seen in historical places. This church was almost as old as the town itself, but the city was bigger now than when he was young, and he was surprised the door still opened when he tried the handle. This was probably the only church still open at night, but with the hospital and the clinic nestled close, it made sense to have a place to sit and think. Birth and death don't stick to banker's hours, and an old church could help earn its keep just by being open when needed. He looked at the shapes in the half dark around him, still feeling the hollowness of his mother's death; the hunger and sadness stirring. This was the first church he remembered: coming here as a family until the third grade, the placid Sunday order put on like the hand-me-down sport coat he wore, moving up the aisle until his father stopped beside a row, standing aside to let the four boys file in. His oldest brother was usually first, with Jake always in the rear, close to his parents, so they could keep an eye on him when he began to fidget. In third grade they'd moved to the new church, the one where they'd just held his mother's funeral. But Jake hadn't forgotten this room, the old church that smelled like his grandmother's house, or the stained-glass window in the wall above the altar.

In those days faith was simple, passed to him whole, like the hand-me-down clothing he wore: a story told by the adults around him. He tried it on and it seemed to fit. But slowly he realized it wasn't completely his, already shaped by the previous owners. When he was too young for a driver's license, he would stop sometimes in the night church, walking home from a movie with friends. It was a quiet place to warm up- talking in the pews, if there were no adults to turn and glare. By then they'd begun to feel the chafe of the larger world, to see cracks in the simple expectations of home, school and childhood. Other energies were looming beneath that facade: whispers of sex, death, chaos and happenstance, the turbulent mysteries of power and blood. It was a darkness they'd always felt but never seen clearly, and now it seemed to be crawling into their flesh; changing their bodies, and making everything more complicated. Of course they were entranced by that darkness, looking into it, while the adults seemed to want to look away. Then this church became a destination in their night wanderings, a place that opened into mystery: safe and scary, dark and comforting, all at the same time.

Every town has its gothic horrors. Not the ones in books or on TV, but the terrible, ordinary things that happen in people's lives. You know. A car full of kids went over that bump – that bump on the park road you're only supposed to go twenty over – and they hit it at sixty, so the car went off the road. But everyone was fine, mostly, except the girl sitting where the car hit the tree. She's alive, but it looks like she'll be in a wheelchair for the rest of her life, and it's hard to understand her when she talks. Things like that happen somewhere every day. But parents seemed to want to forget those stories, to turn away from all that bad luck and ignore it, so maybe it wouldn't rub off. But Jake and his friends needed to look, staring into the darkness here in the night church, drawn to the ragged edge of possibility.

Sometimes, when they opened the outer door, leaves that had pooled on the steps came blasting into the vestibule as they filed in; the wind as restless as the life inside them, slamming the door behind. If there were adults inside, they would talk quietly until the others left, and then the cigarettes came out, tentatively lit and passed from hand to hand, so everyone could have a try. That was a time when such things weren't forbidden, in fact, smoking in public was so common that there were little foil ashtrays in the entryway. Adults were simply required to look after their mess and fold it up in the ashtray, tossing it all in the metal wastebasket on the way out. Of course teenagers were another matter, and Jake and his friends felt like pirates smoking here. But cigarettes were easy to buy, from lonely machines in stairways and hotel lobbies, probably there to encourage new recruits. Still, Jake would always hesitate before dropping his quarters in, until he was sure no one was watching. Walking out with that red and white pack stuffed in his pocket felt like he'd just pulled off a heist. But he always hid the pack in the garage when he went home, since contraband there could be anyone's, with blame likely shifting to older brothers, while a careless bulge in his pocket or smoke on his breath would cause trouble. They'd all decided it was okay to smoke in the night church, God had bigger fish to fry. And somehow that rebellion set the stage for their conversations, a different kind of offering in a different kind of fellowship.

"Did you hear about Gwen's big brother?" Tom asked the question.

"You mean the one who died up North? Near the Boundary Waters?"

"Yeah. But did you hear the real story? I talked to Bobby Fuller at the party after the football game. His brother was there."

"I just know Roger got killed. The car turned over or something. On a gravel road up North." There was an edge of curiosity now. "What happened?"

A pause, making the silence that the story would fill, then the quiet voice: "Bobby said the car flipped over, and everybody got out but Roger. There were five of them. They'd been camping in the Boundary Waters all week and were on their way home. But Roger was pinned. They couldn't get his door open. He was stuck because the seat was bent, and they couldn't move it to get him out the back." Tom took a drag on his cigarette, expelling the smoke dramatically. "They were still trying when the car caught fire. But they couldn't free him or stop the flames, and the heat finally forced them back.

Then they had to listen to his screams. He begged for help until he died. Bobby said his brother started crying when he told the story."

The whistled sound from many mouths. "Jesus!"

There was silence again, while they looked around the church. Then there was another story, and another.

"Did you hear about Jerry Dorset?"

Anne nodded. "Everybody knows about that. He shot himself outside his girlfriend's house, after she broke up with him. They were juniors. She'd started dating someone else."

Rick's face was earnest, he wanted to top that last story. "But did you hear how they found him? He was down in the bushes outside her window..."

"So how'd they find him?"

"It was her dog. Her father let the dog out in the morning, and he was barking by her window, and then he ran back with something in his mouth. Jerry'd used a shotgun..."

"Gross!! Com'on Rick. Jesus!"

"That's what happened!" Rick had gone too far, as usual.

But Anne persisted. "So why didn't they hear?"

"No one was home! And Kristen was out on a date." Rick gestured with his cigarette.

But Jeff was laughing maniacally now, the depth of his reading and his cynicism already precocious. "Wait a minute! If a boyfriend shoots himself outside your window, and no one's there to hear, does it make any sound?"

Disgust on many faces. "Com'on Jeff! The guy's dead. Don't be a jerk!"

And then the sadness that clung to Jeff like a stink these days was shining in his eyes, and then the anger – bright and hot. "He did it to himself!! Over a girl! My cousin got drafted, and someone *there* did it to him, a stranger he didn't even see! In Vietnam."

We nodded at the familiar sadness. Rick put his arm around Jeff. The night church was full of stories then, full of questions. "Do you think there's life on other planets?"

"Did you see the Outer Limits last night? There was this guy who slid down a beam of laser light from out in space, all the way to earth!"

And another night:

"Did you hear what happened to Jeff?"

"Something good I hope." Anne's face was sad.

A smile. "You could say that. Did he tell you about the sleepover at Rob's?"

Shaking heads all-round.

"Good. Then I can tell you. Do you remember Jennifer, Rob's big sister?"

"Of course. Wasn't she homecoming queen once?"

"Well, she's home on break from college."

"I didn't know they were out already."

"Yeah. Jeff didn't know that either."

Now the curiosity again. "What happened?"

"The boys were sleeping in the basement, and Jeff woke up in the middle of the night. He had to pee, so he heads for the bathroom upstairs, but the lights are off and he gets confused. He's walking down this hallway, and he thinks the bathroom's close, when a door opens and light fills the hall. Then Jennifer comes walking out, completely naked, with a towel around her hair. Of course she almost has a heart attack when she sees him, and he's completely embarrassed, apologizing and apologizing, and she says she thought everyone was asleep. But Jeff can't take his eyes off her, she's so beautiful, and then she just laughs at him: she stands there and laughs. Then she lifts her hands and turns in a circle, like she's modeling or something. Then she smiles and heads back to her room. 'Don't worry Jeffrey, you'll get there. But no rush. Enjoy the trip!' That's what she says as she walks past. Then she stops. 'I'm sorry about your cousin. Gary was a really nice guy.' And she walks into her room and closes the door behind her."

"Wow!"

"Oh my God!" Smiles and shaking heads.

"And when she came down to breakfast, she winked at him across the table when no one was looking!"

Laughter. "I always liked Jennifer!"

"If you want to join her fan club, I think Jeff is starting one. He's got a major crush."

Then everyone had to tell their stories, the tales of gratuitous nudity. But Jeff's hand-me-down account was still the best, though you had to know Jennifer to understand. Jake remembered her like a sexy Snow White, or maybe Snow White and the Evil Queen combined. She used to babysit for him and inspired lots of speculation. He even wrote her a poem. She was the muse for his first 'Inferno.'

But this kind of discussion always ended in the same place:

"Who do you think will be first? You know, to go all the way?"

Tom made the nomination. "Probably Jeff. He's already getting a mustache..." Heads nodded. And the motion passed.

Possibility turned in the night church, with stories told in the quiet warmth. When Jake glanced at the window above the altar, the figure there was welcoming and free of judgment. The days passed: time flowing through them all and marking them with change. Then they got their driver's licenses, and the world transformed again.

Now Jake rolled the memories in his mind, savoring the fragments that still lingered here. Alison had mentioned the stained-glass window over dinner, maybe that's why he'd come back to this bench. The faith we hang our lives on starts from simple things. But Jake's faith was more roughly stuck together now, more like the multicolored midden of some burrowing animal than something shaped from any doctrine. Little, shiny bits of meaning were wrapped around his core, a midden of pieces he'd gleaned from his life, that sheltered his days and kept his heart safe. Just a few days ago he was standing in front of a room full of people, trying to sum up a life from the paper in his hands. He was in the new church – where he'd been in the choir and an altar boy long ago – looking out on familiar faces. Standing there, he'd been trying to cope with a feeling that kept breaking through his numbness, a feeling that someone he'd loved all his life had just vanished completely. The shock of it hung in the room. Where's your mom? Gone. Completely gone. A ghost of absence. He read the words he'd written on the paper, because he had to say something, but the faith that he'd shared in that church was transformed in the years since he'd left, and the words couldn't fill the space inside him. Tonight he was back in the old church again, the sanctuary of childhood, chasing more memories. And the window was there, just as Alison had said, high above the altar, and lit from the outside, glowing into the room.

The first time Jake saw that window he was four years old. He was sitting on a wooden bench, with his father on one side and his mother on the other, and his three brothers lined up down the row, all looking nearly tame in their sport coats and ties. Illiterate and impatient, he was glancing down the aisle, waiting for something to happen, unable to jump or run away, penned in the gap between parents. A forest of bodies stretched around him, all moving and talking quietly, like stirring skyscrapers in a great, hushed city, all strangers to him here. There was nothing to look at but people, or the tops of colored-glass stretching up the walls, with bright pictures that made no sense unless you already knew what they were.

But there was a round window above the altar with three children near a seated figure. The man was on a rock at the top of a little hill. He was in profile with the children scattered close; his hand an extended invitation. The face there was welcoming, but strange;

the smile almost sad. There were letters under the picture, but Jake couldn't read – one of the many doors closed to him then – but this was clearly a picture from some story, like a page from a book at home, and he wanted to know what the story was.

Jake wondered sometimes if they put it there on purpose, knowing that window was all children could see during the service, or if it just happened when they built the church. He spent hours over many Sundays looking at that picture, waiting through the ritual and trying to understand what was going on around him. He'd look at the greens and blues of the landscape inside the glass, wondering what was past the rock the man was sitting on. If you could roll down that hill, what was at the bottom? Was there water? Maybe a lake or a stream you could wade in? And if you picked up a stone to skip in that stream, would it have the same blue-brown color that the rock did? Would the whole landscape have those colors, if you could step through the window into that world? And Jake wondered where the dogs were. They must be running on the grassy hill or swimming in the stream. There had to be dogs if there were children outside – that was just a fact of life. Jake's mother always said she could tell where he was just by looking down the block. Their old Dalmatian would be sleeping on the lawn near whichever house he was in. The dog was just waiting for them to come back outside, so she could rejoin the game.

Of course Jake learned who the man was when he asked about the window, but he had trouble with the inscription. His mom said the words were from the Bible: "Suffer the children to come unto me." But Jake didn't see why anyone wanted children to suffer. She'd explained it was an old way of speaking, that 'suffer' just meant 'allow,' and Jesus was saying it was okay for the children to talk to him; they weren't bothering him or anything, he wanted to see them. Jake thought that was pretty nice, since Jesus was so important and everything. Adults seemed to spend most of their time ignoring kids, when they weren't telling them what to do. The man in the window looked like he'd listen.

So faith was born in Jake's childhood soul, an inkling of greater things whispered in colored glass. And sometimes, when something was happening in the church and everyone stood, his father lifted Jake on his shoulders to see. Then Jake was the tallest in the room, sitting there straddling his father's head, with an ear in each hand. Though he didn't really understand what was happening around him, the exaltation was wonderful. Jake liked it best when everyone was marching; especially when they were marching out, lining up in that double file, with the choir and the minister so energetic in their robes, so righteous and happy, while everybody sang. It was always best at the end, when it was almost time to go home.

Childhood was a wonderful place, embedded in his family and looking out on an orderly world. When they'd moved, the stained-glass window stayed behind with that part of his childhood. But, though the words and the rituals meant little to him then, it was the image in the window that he'd taken with him from that place, an icon of a fatherly God, almost a big brotherly God: that picture was something he understood. It was like part of his family, or a piece of a dream; living just on the edge of sleep, where the world opened into a strange blue landscape.

When Jake and his friends were in the night church, Jesus was up there on the glass, watching them through the corner of his eye as he beckoned the children. His face was welcoming and free of judgment; even to the smokers there crashing the event. "Suffer the children to come unto me." Sometimes they talked about that. Did 'suffer' have two meanings in the inscription? Because none of them were very happy, and something was always wrong somewhere. Now there was real darkness on the edges of their lives, and real choices to be made. The world was a complicated place. But that wasn't the only thing happening in their lives: as the darkness came into focus around them, so did the beauty.

Alison had mentioned the window at dinner because he'd taken her to see it once. That was back in high school, after they'd been going out for three months. They'd been to a movie downtown and were walking and talking through the winter cold, with no money for restaurant seating. But neither seemed to feel the chill, warmed by the fire they were making between them, walking and talking close. A restlessness had gotten in their legs and neither wanted to go back to the car and drive to Tina's party, both content with present company. For Jake this was all completely new. He'd never known anyone who could listen so carefully and then catch the thread and take it somewhere else, making it blossom into something they had shaped between them like nothing either could have made alone. Talking with Alison was as much fun as kissing her, or just walking beside her holding hands. It was amazing, this addition of one plus one, making a fire that lifted both up, making them shine. Looking into his eyes and leaning close, Alison laughed and put her arms around him when he tried to explain that feeling. Usually the family car was their boudoir, when Jake could wrangle it, a movable feast parked in lonely places. They already began to explore each other's bodies, placing flags on unconquered landscape all over their adolescent flesh. But that night they were walking in the cold with no destination, and then the night church was on the corner, shining softly in the dark. Jake decided to show her the window, and they went inside.

It had been empty, so they walked up and sat on the floor in the chancel with their backs against the choir stalls, looking up through the gated sanctuary at the window above the altar. Jake told her the story, kissing and talking there, feeling the audacity of their presence in this sacred space. But it didn't feel like desecration, more like they were bringing something sacred with them, out of the night and into the church, mussing the hair of a stodgy simplicity to bring a vital freshness in. "Suffer the children to come unto me." Jesus said it and they took him at his word.

Alison had laughed at Jake, at that grumpy boy sitting on the hard bench, looking up at the window or paging through prayer books he couldn't read. Where were all the pictures? He assured her that by the time his family left this church he could read just fine, and she laughed, kissing him again, warm lips on his face. And as Jake rocked back from that sharing he glanced up at the window, but now its mood seemed completely changed.

Now the figure there seemed to be smiling. He was almost sly, and His eyes were radiant: 'I told you it would get better! That you wouldn't wait on that bench forever!' Though the profile was unchanged, the figure seemed to be spreading his arms to the children before him, offering the world: "This beauty is boundless!" This was new to Jake, a faith where love and sex were also sacraments, where the delicious otherness of relation made living complete. "Here is the feast, here is the sweetness!" Life was being offered from His extended hands, and it was wholly beautiful. "Suffer the children to come unto me." Here is the gift. Take it and eat.

And Jake had tried to explain that vision to Alison, sitting in the chancel, talking and kissing, telling stories of their families and growing up in this town. They'd wandered out of the church that night closer than when they'd gone inside.

Now Jake rocked slowly in the dark pew, waking that habit from childhood, losing himself in memories. He was smiling. Alison had reminded him of that night at dinner, of the innocence and tenderness between them then. They'd shared a smile across the table, and she'd reached to hold his hand. They were so much older now, and so much better protected. It was all water under the bridge, but that night had been a wonderful moment in their time together.

Soon enough there'd been another night, the flip side of the first.

Home for Christmas, a freshman in college, Jake had sought out the window again. First love had collapsed in painful confusion, though Alison had warned him things would change if he left. She wanted him to stay close to home, but he wanted to be out in the wider world. So she'd changed things with the same dramatic flair she brought to most of her life. They'd made plans, of course, to be apart for two years and then transfer to the same school, getting married when they graduated. At first they'd written letters nearly every day, talking on the phone when they could. But Alison had warned him. And it turned out love was just a feeling after all, an idea that had gotten in their flesh, sweeping them up, only to vanish when circumstances changed. Like an exquisite Humpty Dumpty, love was balanced precariously between them, and when it was broken and empty on the ground, neither could make it whole again. After all their wrangling, Alison had made things clear by sleeping with one of his friends. She was looking for something new with some-one who'd stayed in town, while giving him that metaphoric middle finger over her shoulder. It was happening everywhere freshman year, but this was Jake's first heartbreak; the first that went deep, and fierce as any pain he'd felt. So he'd come back to the night church to file a complaint. Downtown with friends, he'd decided to walk home alone, and when he saw the familiar building he remem-bered why. He had a bone to pick with an icon there, and Jake had gone inside.

But this time the church wasn't empty. There was a couple in the front row kneeling, whispering into folded hands; so Jake sat in the back, trying not to intrude. Though he gazed around the familiar space, it was hard not to be drawn to the couple in front; something was clearly happening there. After kneeling for many minutes, the two sat back and folded the pads under their seat. Then the man leaned close, speaking quietly. But the woman silenced him, putting her hand across his lips. But he took her hand and held it softly, continuing, saying something Jake couldn't hear. Now the woman was shaking her head and trying to move her hand back over his mouth. And then she was weeping. And then she was sobbing, throwing her arms around the man's neck and sobbing against his chest. He held her there, rocking gently while she cried against him. And as the stranger held her, stroking her hair with his fingers, the tenderness between them reminded Jake of his own sadness, and he felt the tears begin to rise. Crying was something he'd tried to put away, banished by more adult aspirations, but it returned abruptly. Feeling the love between the strangers in the front, he sobbed quietly in the back, silently sharing their pain. When the couple had finally calmed, they stood up briskly and strode past him down the aisle. Jake nodded as they passed, but they were already somewhere else, steeled for what was coming, decisions made and features set. After sitting for a moment, Jake moved to the front, looking up at that familiar window.

The mood on the glass was different now, the sadness had returned to edge the smile on the figure's face. Young Jake moved to get a better look, sitting down in the chancel where they'd sat two years ago. The crying helped; he felt much better. And his problem was much simpler than what those strangers must be facing. He guessed they'd gone back to the hospital to confront what was waiting. Looking up, the window changed.

All the beauty shining there on the winter night with Alison hadn't gone away, but now the sadness he'd just witnessed had been drawn into it, like the sadness and the beauty created something else. He stared at that enigmatic smile, the hands that offered life and the children gathered close. Jake shook his head. It was beautiful and complicated, the darkness and the light so close together now, the beauty and the pain so closely mixed. He looked at the face again and realized that was the only answer he was going to get.

So he'd wiped his own face, stood up in the dark, and finished his walk home.

Now an older Jake is sitting in the night church, looking up at that familiar window, rocking slowly in the pew. Both his parents are dead, and his brothers are getting old. Many of the friends he knew here have scattered across the country, and many are already gone. Alison keeps in touch, the remains of love still whispering between them, like some dwarf star left spinning in the dark long after its supernova, and through the years those remnants have warmed, and they've become good friends. With kids mostly grown and divorces to hash over, there's plenty to talk about whenever he's in town. Now it's almost time to head back to his brother's house, and pick up his son. Jake looks at the window again, feeling the ache, missing the parents that sat beside him here. It's part of a mystery he no longer tries to understand. And the figure smiles sadly from the glass, His hands an invitation, while the children are scattered close.

You Rock-Cracking Rock-Cracker, Looking for Bones,

Alicia Tebeau-Sherry

you're still with me.
Out in the backyard you
pound feet like slick Gannets
fishing for the only place
grass grows & when you
reach it, cozumel arms stretch
up between your toes as
you crouch above prey set
just before the river
rocks circling the tree
& the frog-pond Mom
made from concrete &

moss mosaic. I sway with

the way your honey-blonde
bangs mingle with your
eyelashes, spotting sun in &
out of vision as you roll a
heavy handful like a marble
game onto your chosen
platform—a bigger
rock. Then you rip the
sheet from cadaver-bumps

& you take an everyday
fruit-sized rock & place
the others dripping sunlight
upon the stage like they are
in for a head-chopping,
& they are in a sense, but
with six-year-old intentions,
& you dive, like teeth
into apples & oranges. You
breathe & blow away shards,

& your dusty eyes drool at
the cracks & clashes. One
hand & one rock become
a gavel, a Gannet, fruit falling
from a tree & come down like
weight & points & you grin
like any six-year-old at the
ordinary rock that somehow
looks different split open.
You were looking for bones.

O' six-year-old self,
O' little paleontologist,
O' digger & diver,
O' cracker & crasher,
O' little, vast mind,
you're still with me.
—it's just that now
my rocks sound
like pencil-tips breaking,
plastic pens snapping,
keyboard keys collapsing,
& they look more like heads.

Untangled from Our Strawberry Nets

Alicia Tebeau-Sherry

you were cold. You
nudged. I balled
my hands. You
attempted a jump—
I gripped you
like I was warming
the moon. I'm not

the sun—I learned
that ducklings need
100 watt lamps, not open
bowls of water to dampen
in overnight. I've held
death—a dandelion
with its head popped

off, a cracked egg's
slime, a sheet of bamboo
toilet paper—but I'd never held
something dying by mistake
until now—the stiffening
of fluff. I shouldn't
have watched your eyes.

Corrections

Kit Storjohann

"Why did you leave?"

"You asked me to."

Her response, despite her absence, has become sacramental in its repetition over the years. The phantasmal image of my wife, summoned to answer my question yet again, disappears as abruptly as its corporeal counterpart once did. I rest my head against the window, letting the frost-chilled glass find a dozen tiny, invisible cuts across my forehead into which to sink its icy bite.

The day on the other side is incongruously bright and sunny, and my neighbor builds his wall on the boundary between our properties. The scruffy, taciturn man (whose name I can never recall) is piling stones the size of dictionaries onto one another, laboriously lacing them into a bulwark against uncorralled grass. I offer a friendly wave, but he is suddenly gone; both of our yards are coated in snow, with only an ankle-high mound marking his progress.

"You keep referring to it as a recent event," the therapist says.

She roosts in her chair across the room, trying not to shift around despite her obvious nervousness. "But it's been six years since the accident."

Her home office is decorated to saccharine excess. Floor-to-ceiling windows spill sunlight across homemade paintings of butterflies, photographs of waterfalls, and inspirational phrases in cartoonish letters—all of which imply that my time as her unenthusiastic charge could be truncated through sheer will. I struggle out of the quaggy grip of the couch and start to pace.

"Yeah, but who's counting?" I ask as I circle her office. "You know how much I enjoy our little talks together. What's a few revolutions around the sun between old chums, hmm?"

She sets pad and pen in her lap to adjust the tiny round frames of her glasses with pinched thumb and forefinger. "This is our first session," she says. "We met for the first time about half an hour ago."

My stride does not falter in the face of this naked dissemblance. The birds on her perfectly manicured lawn flutter from perch to perch, prompted by a frenetic mix of whim and unease. She lives well for a "caring healer." I wonder if she considers her efforts at alleviating suffering to cancel out her husband's merciless business dealings, which keep the pair in this splendor. I have thoroughly researched both of them. At the moment, however, trotting out damning facts about him would come off as a cheap, desperate distraction from her awkward gambit.

"You've tried to convince me of that before," I say. "Not that I fault you for attempting this approach. I'm sure these unorthodox techniques tend to work on many people. Bombard them with flagrant lies until they start to doubt their own reality. Then you can mold them as you see fit. But I think you'll find that I'm not as susceptible as most; I'm almost certainly smarter than you."

In the ensuing swath of silence, she studies her notes. "Well," she says finally. "Your academic achievements certainly are formidable, more on par with a college professor than a former high school history teacher. And your IQ is higher than normal—"

"Bordering on genius."

"Mmm," she agrees with an unenthusiastic nod. "But that alone doesn't always make you right."

"Of course not. But it does mean that I have a greater chance of knowing what I'm talking about than...most people."

"Mmm. But are you, perhaps, being so hostile to the therapeutic process because you're afraid of venturing into an arena where you might not be 'right' all of the time?"

"Clumsy attempt at transition there, Doc. Oh, I forgot," I say, snapping my finger with feigned recollection. "You're not a doctor—I am. But, to be honest, it's not much comfort being 'right' about anything. If the rest of the world remains deluded then you're just dismissed as a madman or a fool.

"For instance," I continue, stopping my pacing and sliding into lecture mode, complete with gesticulations. "If I were to tell you that the square root of two-hundred-eighty-nine is seventeen, but you say it's sixteen, then nothing I can say or show you is going to convince you otherwise. You'll even go so far as to tell me the calculator is broken before admitting you're wrong."

"Mmm," she says. "But the square root of two-hundred-fifty-six actually is sixteen."

"I said two-hundred-eighty-nine," I correct her, undaunted by her ability to solve an equation — albeit the wrong one—without resorting to scribbling on her pad.

"I'm fairly certain you're wrong," she says, her pompous grin stretching from one face-framing drape of gray hair to the other. "We can all be wrong from time to time."

"Well, one of us is," I say, resuming my orbit. "But I do know that I've been here before."

"When was that?"

"What do you mean, when? The last time."

"Just once?"

"No." I have unwittingly allowed annoyance to creep into my voice. I stop walking, gaze at the ceiling, and draw breath through my teeth with great deliberation. When I turn to face her, I repay her condescension in kind, enunciating every word as though scolding a child. "We have a standing appointment which I do not enjoy, but I never miss. And we always discuss the same things. You keep telling me I'm not as smart as I think I am, and that we've never done this before. You ask about why I chose to teach high school and what made me stop teaching. And yet you treat me as though I'm just showing up on your doorstep for the first time like a timid prom date. I'm not some stammering beau clutching a rose, my dear, and you've no need to play the coquette with me. Not only are we both old hands at these steps, but we've danced together many times before."

"Mmm. Do you think I'm trying to be romantic with you?"

"Oh for Christ's sake, Doc! Or counselor, or guru, or whatever you call yourself. It's just a figure of speech. An extended metaphor, if you will. I know you have a penchant for poetry."

"What makes you say that?"

"'Two paths diverged in a yellow wood,'" I floridly spout. "You've said before that it's one of your favorites, but I think you missed the point of the poem. Everyone misses the point. One would think you would have outgrown those stale quotes from the yearbook moldering in the attic."

"It is one of my favorites," she unabashedly admits. "But I don't think you remember discussing it with me. I think you noticed the framed copy on the wall." A sausage-plump finger waves behind her towards a woodland scene of a forked path overlaid with the Frostian inscription.

"Of course I've noticed. We've discussed it many times."

"And what do you think that I think it's about?"

"Do we really need to play this game?"

"Please," she says. "Indulge me." My newborn mission is to water the tiny seed of irritation I hear beneath her voice. Her forced calm and manufactured kindness has pitilessly grated on me over the time we've spent "working" together, and this little gap in her defenses can and shall be exploited to its fullest potential. "Tell me what I think the poem means."

"All your life you've been a truly unique individual," I chant, my singsongy tone out-Heroding Herod. "You've never just been a part of the crowd. No, you've followed your own passions, blazed a trail. You—a radiant, unique soul—have forged your own path through this world: the road less traveled. And that has made all the difference. It's made you the wonderful and special and fully actualized individual that you are." I cap the mocking homily with a smirk.

"And what do you think the poem means?"

I sit down on the couch again, more exhausted than I thought I was. "I think it's about..." I say airily, pausing dramatically before I gruffly blurt: "Bullshit! I think we make up bullshit, then smear it all over everything, roll around in it, and get absolutely filthy. I think Frost saw how we get obsessed with all the petty minutiae and how important we think it is, and he decided to chide us. In the end it makes no difference which road you choose: You'll secretly pine for the one you didn't take, yet manage to convince yourself you were right all along. We'll tell ourselves that we followed our heart, that we're actually happy — even if we feel miserable and powerless."

"And do you feel miserable and powerless?"

"No," I say. "Just annoyed."

"Mmm. And what road do you lament not taking?"

"Are you paid by the question?"

"Well, that's witty evasion. Are you afraid to answer?"

"I have already answered that question. Many times. Oh, yes, I forgot. We're playing our usual parts of eyelash-batting virgins to the therapy game, right? Well, then: I wish I hadn't had the accident."

"I don't think," she says, "that constitutes a road not taken. You get to choose the form and pace of your recovery. To wish the accident itself away is an exercise in futility."

"This whole process is an exercise in futility," I say, realizing that I am suddenly and inexplicably enervated. "Maybe if I had done one little thing differently..." The gravity in my tone surprises me. "If I'd left a few minutes earlier. Taken a different route. Things wouldn't have happened the way they did. My career wouldn't have been sabotaged and destroyed. My wife would never have left me. I wouldn't ache like an old man. I'd be strong enough," I say, "to help my neighbor finish his wall."

"Wall?" she asks, rolling it around in her mouth like a foreign word.

"Yes. He's building a wall. Property marker. You know: 'Good walls make good neighbors' for the irony-deaf crowd."

"And you want to help him build his wall?"

"I'm curious about it. He's got this system where he uses a mud paste as mortar. He mixes in all sorts of seeds and nutrients, and he claims that this concoction will grow moss and ivy to help the rocks bond together. Personally I doubt it will work — mosses and lichens tend to hold in moisture, which can damage stone over time. At the rate he's going, we'll both be moss ourselves before he finishes."

"And you want to build things? Build walls perhaps?"

"I just want something to do, other than wonder where everything went. And have the same conversations about it over and over."

Although I'm playing up my exasperation for her benefit, I truly am tired of the routines that have gnawed my days into monotony. I can perfectly recall the many times we've sat in this office rehashing the same conversation, yet I have the bus number circled on the schedule in my pocket in case I forget it. Some things grow tedious, others unfathomably alien.

On my walks into town, I sometimes wonder about the disappearance of the boy down the street. I used to pass him almost every afternoon; he would stand in the driveway trying to flip his skateboard over and land on it again. With the solemnity of a martial arts student punching a board thousands of times in the hopes of breaking it someday, he focused on mastering this pointless trick. I would tap my fingers to the brim of my hat, and he would return my salute with that earnest jocularity that only a ten-year-old boy can muster.

At some point after I'd begun huffing and puffing my way through my route, he vanished from his driveway. His family's house descended into its current state of dilapidation (complete with flaking paint, missing storm doors, and a weed-choked yard) with astounding rapidity. In his place there are now three pale, ratty, blond-haired toddlers of indeterminate gender, staring at me like something from a horror film. I assume that the boy's mother is minding these urchins for someone else, but neither she nor my young friend is anywhere to be seen. Instead, a skeletal man stands a few feet away watching me as though I am about to lurch forward, scoop up one of the hideous children, and carry it off.

Aside from the bus ride to the therapist's home office and my (more or less) daily walks, I have little need to leave the house. Most of my time is spent cross-referencing my voluminous notes, many of which I no longer recall writing. Yet the handwriting is undeniably mine, as is the thought process that made those insights and connections. They might be fragments of a time before the accident, relics of the man I used to be. But they continue to proliferate, the ink sometimes so fresh that it smears. My pen has been unwittingly fecund since my accident.

"You aren't yourself," my wife had said right after I returned home from the hospital.

"A few bones to mend," I'd answered. "Some cuts to heal. Other than that, I'm more myself than ever."

"No, you're not. Something's changed."

"If anything has changed," I said, "it is that I no longer have time to waste with silly questions. I've simply lost the patience to suffer fools gladly."

"You never had that much patience to begin with."

"Well, then fools of the world: Beware!"

I have the distinct impression that I inherited this house; I certainly have no recollection of buying it. There should be scenes in my mind of my wife and I discovering this rustic outpost, of appeals to banks, of signing on dotted lines, but I have none of these memories. Nor can I recall ever paying mortgage or rent or even taxes. I am certain that I did not grow up here, but I recall the time before my neighbor and his fledgling wall arrived.

Dozens of places where I've lived come swimming up to the fore of my mind when I think of the word "home." From cozy, firelit houses to the transient hovels of graduate school penury. A few have been shared with my wife, some with other people—other women, friends, roommates whose faces I see clearly but whose names I cannot recall. I remember almost every word of my PhD thesis verbatim, but have no recollection of the place where I wrote it.

This house itself is occasionally mysterious. Little alcoves will suddenly appear where I have not seen them before. Wood-paneled walls are drying out and decaying in haste, and I curse the shoddy workmanship of whatever forgotten soul is responsible. Wallpaper peels and bubbles and I promise myself that I shall repair it some-day. The bathroom—poorly grouted with buckling tiles and creeping patches of mold—serves its function well enough. The roof, mercifully, does not leak when it rains, and I have ample room for all of my books and papers.

Almost every room is festooned with boxes, file cabinets, and bookshelves. The organizational system (which I cannot imagine having devised) could most charitably be described as abstract. Yet I always manage to find what I need. One of the storage areas was presumably intended as a bedroom, but my nights are spent falling asleep on the couch with the lights still on, my face mashed into the pages while I wander through dreams that I never remember.

My kitchen is functional, but mostly neglected. The little market in town provides me with enough in the way of breads, fruits, cold cuts, and the like to keep me alive and thriving. I have no skill as a gourmet, and my wife's various pots and cooking apparatuses—their functions specialized to the point of uselessness—sleep undisturbed in the cabinets.

I walk down my dirt driveway and onto the street as many days as I can manage it, regardless of the weather. In one direction lies the main street in all of its faux-Americana glory. In the other stand unclaimed and untamed fields closed with wildflowers, spilling off into distant copses of trees. Sometimes I will venture into the bosom of nature and find myself marveling at a tiny spider web or the curl of a leaf. But most days I stroll into town, waving to neighbors who seem to change faces more often than I change my socks. My wife was the one who was good at keeping up with who was who, and she left me adrift when I was too broken to protest.

"That was decades ago," my therapist says with a lilt of surprise in his voice when I speak of my wife's departure.

I smile at his feigned innocence. Sitting on the floor of his unconventional office in what was once called Indian-style but now inexplicably takes its name from applesauce, he frequently strokes his long beard in an affectation of thoughtfulness. Untouched strands vibrate sympathetically and give the impression that some unseen creature nests below his chin. Aside from the thread of incense spiraling towards the ceiling, the air in the room is perfectly still, yet wisps of his long hair quiver in some undetectable breeze. Despite his attempt to appear as a wizened sage, he is probably young enough to have been one of my students.

"I believe your time frame is slightly off there, Doc," I say.

"Oh?"

"The accident was only a few years ago. That's when the wheels came off, if you'll pardon the inadvertent association. We've discussed this many times: The accident happened, my job was unjustly taken away, and my wife left. That's why I've been coming to see you over the last couple of years."

"But it hasn't been a 'couple of years,'" he says in a soft, patronizing voice. "We've only begun our work recently. And the accident you keep alluding to happened much longer ago than that."

"We have been going over this for the last few years," I reply, stressing the final words for emphasis. "Why are you continually trying to convince me that we're veritable strangers to each other?"

"Well, I wouldn't go so far as to say strangers," he says in his soulful stew of confusion and unearned arrogance. It might have served him well had he chosen to host a children's television show, but undercuts his current efforts. "But we've only had a few sessions together."

"Not this again. Have you forgotten everything we've ever talked about?"

"I remember our conversations. But you tend not to talk about yourself all that much. We spent much of our last session chatting about String Theory."

He'd learned, from reading an article that was simplified beyond the point of what an adult should find acceptable, that tiny strings vibrated. I'd had to clarify that we observe only a very small fraction of a single order of magnitude, and need to extrapolate from that little sliver of reality based on models. I'd begun to walk him through the math that was now making these models something more concrete than blind, poetic stabs at the air until his eyes glazed over. "I am an educated and curious man, Doctor. I am a doctor too, you know."

"Yes," he says, magnanimously agreeing to recognize what he doubtlessly considers a lesser course of study than the one that allegedly gives his mumblings their undue authority. "You have a PhD in medieval English history, I understand."

"My doctoral thesis was on the evolution of currency in 10th century Anglo-Saxon Britain."

"Yet in our few sessions together we've discussed quantum physics, Apache folklore, experimental neurobiology, the impact of Caravaggio, and the legal reforms of the Qin Empire."

"Everything is connected. If you pursue any thread it will eventually intersect with every other one. Besides," I say. "They're all subjects I find fascinating. One should never stop learning."

"Well, I'm in agreement with you on that. But I think you might be trying to deflect the conversation away from yourself. You try to prove that you're overqualified for the position you used to have. You keep claiming that your job was 'unjustly taken' from you. But, according to the records, that's not what happened."

"Then what happened?"

"The record states," he says, clumsily adding a pause to manufacture suspense, "that you became violent towards a student."

"That didn't happen."

"The reports say that you began behaving erratically in the classroom. That you had started rambling incoherently, and stopped being able to remember your students' names."

"Students come and go. I tend to ramble. It is actually one of my more charming attributes — if you bothered to ask the better strain of my former students. A lot of people have told me that what they remember most about high school was Crazy Doc Kunsmauer's Western Civ class," I tell him. "They remembered the salacious anecdotes I told about royal sex lives, and silly pneumonic devices like Phil the Phoenician inventing cuneiform. Its value might elude the closed-minded," I say, gesturing toward him, "but acting a little bit crazy is a very useful pedagogical tool. It keeps the students engaged and alert."

"Your behavior was described as more than 'a little bit crazy.' You started ranting and yelling in class."

"I always ranted and yelled. You have to get them excited again after television has dulled their minds. You can't teach them if they're falling asleep, and you can't get kids to relate to The Munster Rebellion unless you compare it to Waco. Get them feeling for people over four hundred years ago by relating it to something that just happened."

"Just happened," he repeats softly. "From what my records say, you became verbally abusive towards your students. You also began jabbering and yelling incoherently." When I remain silent, he continues. "They claimed that by the end you weren't even talking in complete sentences anymore, and some people thought you'd lapsed into a foreign language."

"I speak several. But I don't like to show off."

"The pivotal incident was when you started beating a student with your fists." When this calumny fails to elicit a response, he asks, "Does that sound familiar?"

"This conversation certainly sounds familiar, since we've had it many, many times before. But no: that 'incident' did not happen."

"A room full of students and a district observer say it did."

"Well I say it didn't."

"Hmmm. Now, all of this was after you returned to work following your accident?"

"They just used that as an excuse. 'Doc Kunsmauer has gone nuts from brain damage' or something. Sheer nonsense."

"So you believe this was a conspiracy?"

"No," I say with a sigh. "I don't believe in conspiracies, per se. I've told you that many times before. For years now I have been coming here, sitting on this floor with you like a child, and telling you the same stories over and over again."

"Years?"

"Yes."

"How many years?"

"I don't know. Probably five years or so. What does it matter?"

"Why is that question prompting such hostility?"

"Because I'm sure you know the answer, right down to the exact day and time, and I'm sick and tired of playing these games."

"If the incident on record never happened, then why were you fired?"

"Some of the spoiled kids wanted better grades handed to them. Their parents demanded that their little angels be rewarded for their mere existence. The other faculty members didn't want to put in the same effort that I did; they just wanted to punch in and punch out while reading off the answer key. The district didn't like me eliding the curriculum with the complicated truth. So when they found a way to get rid of me, they did. Then they covered their tracks, and probably even convinced themselves that I actually had done those terrible things. Weak minds are malleable in regards to memory."

"Do you know how people construct memories?" my therapist asks. She is younger than her sallow face might lead one to believe. Her ubiquitous scarf, twisted around her head like a turban, covers a scalp I have seen only once or twice. It was ravaged by some trauma that left her hairless and scarred. I enjoy speaking to her, watching her birdlike face stiffen as she listens, recording everything on some mental list with the same decisiveness as a pharaonic scribe. Her voice betrays a considerable effort put into every word she speaks. She has obviously known great pain in her thirty-some-odd years in this world, and it has tempered her into something so hideous that it is beautiful.

My own body has begun to fail prematurely as well, every movement adding unlived decades to the aggregation of my aches. I stopped celebrating birthdays some years back, so I'm not sure of my exact age, but I am probably barely into my forties. Yet joints rankle in pain, and my skin is furrowed with networks of wrinkles. Dark, sagging pouches hang like bats beneath my eyes. I find myself worn and frail without having lived the years to get to this sorry state.

"We have gone over this before," I say.

"My apologies if I don't remember," she replies. "I'm afraid I'll have to ask you to repeat yourself. Do you know how we construct memories?"

"Yes." Honesty always wins points with me, so I repeat my lesson. "Neural pathways are formed in our brains, which chemically encode our perceptions of our experiences. Whenever we wish to access these memories, we activate the pathways, filling our conscious minds with what's been stored there.

"But, there's a catch, of course. We don't remember events as much as we remember our experience of those events. Our mind fills in a lot of blanks, plays with what happened, and shifts things around to make sense. To make our memories tell the stories we want them to tell. And, like a cassette tape, they get worn down as we play them over and over. We don't remember reality; we remember what we've already remembered. And the truth decays. Like copying the cassette over and over again."

"So the more we remember the past, the more we change it. Correct?"

"You've got it," I say.

"Is it possible that you've been working from faulty memories?

That you've worn the...cassettes out? Especially in the decades since your old accident?"

"It's only been a few years," I say.

"Much more than a few."

"It's strange."

"What is?"

"I know that we've had this conversation many times, but I don't recall this part of it."

"How many times?"

"Oh, I don't know. Between two hundred ten and two hundred twenty, I suppose."

"And what have you learned in that time?"

"I have learned that you choose not to see things the way they happened," I say. "And that you've spent an enormous amount of energy trying to convince me that I don't know what I know."

Her eyes lock onto mine and do not let go, her gaze as relentless as the rest of her. I don't think I could have stayed with a therapist without her steely mannerisms for very long—but, since she's the only one I've ever had, the speculation is irrelevant. "Why did your wife leave?" she asks me.

"Because I lost my job."

"But spouses lose jobs all of the time. Why did that prompt such a dramatic reaction?"

"You'd have to ask her."

"Was she the kind of person who would just abandon you without any explanation like that? Over an admittedly painful, but relatively routine, life event?"

"I wouldn't have thought so."

"What would you say to her if she were here right now?"

"The same thing that I've said countless times before."

"Let's try an exercise," my therapist says. As I stare back into her eyes, they stay locked open with impossible rigidity. I realize that I have never seen her blink. Obviously she must do so, and I wonder if it's possible that we blink in unison so that I never notice. "Pretend that she's here. That you're speaking to her just like you're speaking to me. What do you say to her?"

"This hasn't changed since the last time we did this."

"What do you say to her?"

"I ask, 'Why did you leave?'" I face the ghost standing before me in my house. The place looks worse than ever. My tiny lapses in housekeeping have somehow metastasized into utter ruin. Wallpaper has peeled away in strips and lies on the floor like the lifeless wings of butterflies after a frost. Floorboards have separated and frayed into sawdust. The almost charming mustiness has been subsumed within an aggressive stench of mold and rot. I am needled by spears of drafts. The accrued detritus of many snows and thaws has piled atop the window glass into a grotesque patina. I stand before my wife, who I have conjured out of the mists of memory. She is the only thing in the house that has not been aged out of recognition.

"You asked me to."

"I never wanted you to leave," I protest, but she is gone. My hands ache, and I look down at mottled, wrinkled claws which appear as though they burned down to the bone without my noticing. A cough works its way out of my lungs through herculean effort and then lands against the window, flecking the grime-encrusted glass with yellowish spittle and a tinge of cloudiness. My inhalation sounds as though it is being squeezed through a narrow tube. I raise the hand I no longer recognize and wipe the small patch of opacity aside. On the other side of the window, my neighbor's wall has grown to the height of a man, with moss in every visible crevice and cascading ivy so hearty that no more than a stray patch of stone can be seen.

Where We Found Spring

Libby VanBuskirk

We paddled near the past
event
the fallen maple
long in length lying in lake water
trunk severed and bent
orange insides stripped and spilling
but still
blooming baby green
spring leaves.

Only the mountains
would have witnessed the ferocity.
But today we were part of
our own occasion--
he with his camera
    I with notebook and pen.
We longed to pull close, touch

the forsaken tree
but stopped
before a spread-out thin pollen island
attached to the fallen tree
like a cobweb
excessively anchored.

We could not be the knife
to cut the golden floating cover,
not a solid weaving
but the thinnest cloth of unconnected dots,
fresh-fallen, amply clustered
on the cold and quiet lake.
We paused beside
this delicate tribute to spring,
which some time soon
would surely wobble
out of our shared time.

Children of Midnight

Libby VanBuskirk

Silent lake   night still warm.
Midnight. Out I am
in dusky fog   alone.

In the wild cove nearby
the uptick of water   oars splashing? Swimmers?
Too still for waves. No one nearby.
Who's out? Who's there? No answer.

Through overgrown reeds
and washed-in leaves
a boat   full of children drifts in.

    Are they—? Could they be
    our children   his and mine? Our three?

But younger. It cannot be. So many.
Yes. They're ours   our children at every age
as they were-—
        then and then and then   toddlers and ten-year-olds
little and big   dozens. How well I know
that plump little arm   the careful hand steadying
a gunnel, a little body bailing,
and a profiled face just changed by puberty.
I know all—sundry excitements
the face raised to starlight, the long tangled hair.
        By time so long ago dispersed.

I want to pull in their boat. But I'm slow.
The craft scrapes bottom. Children race
beyond the beach   under the first trees
almost to the little woods. They scramble
with flashlights   creating each other from darkness.
Fireflies flash too   in and out of tall grass.

The littlest hide   fitting themselves behind trees.
Others run—searching for old havens?
Who's it? Who's it?
Fast moving beams scribble up and down trees.

I flash my light up too.
What are they looking for?
Chipmunks they loved to notice? Flying squirrels?

By the water some children dig
with quick children's hands   the rusting spade.
Sand flies up. Digging or building as they used to

until they too soon are running.
Finally my feet let me race after them all.
How gently I call
how gently they disappear.

Perfect Excuse

Thomas Benz

Preparations were already underway for their daughter Nell's third birthday, which Hannah seemed eager to fete with the pomp of a royal ball. Laird understood such events were important to his wife. They were the necessary recompenses for all the drudgery and isolation of caring for a young child, a celebration of the experience's trials and wonders. Seduced by elaborate invitations, friends and relatives would soon be converging on the house as if the earth's magnetic fields had shifted to draw them there.

Though the party was still a few weeks off, Laird was going at their considerable lawn with a kind of urgency, just thinking about the errands he still needed to run. A balky shelf kept threatening to slip a hinge and fall on the sofa, and the stroller had lost a wheel. The house needed to be spruced up in myriad ways, and the gladiolas just inside the picket fence looked ready to give up the ghost in the recent heat wave. After refereeing a war the kids waged inside, Hannah called out over the rumble of the mower, "great job honey but don't forget that chipped paint on the gate, and somehow we've got to organize the garage. It looks like a bomb went off."

He glanced over at its contents – boxes of every shape and dimension, bikes lying haphazardly like the aftermath of a tidal wave, rakes, a mangled soccer net — and had to agree. But in the dense air, it seemed beyond him just then: something more suited to the Army Corps of Engineers. "Ok, then I'll build a couple pyramids after that," he muttered toward the screened window though he knew the comment wouldn't reach her, and that he was talking to himself.

"What, Laird?"

"No problem," he shouted, as he hit a snag in the grass that stopped him dead in his tracks.

It was around that time that Laird heard his old classmate Everett Whitmore was in town for some reason. Though the end of summer rush had taken its toll, Laird was determined to see him – if only for a quick drink – and resolve if everything he remembered was true. Everett had seen his share of scrapes (more than his share): the kind where he had to crawl out a back window, or keep a few basic elements of disguise in the trunk of his car. Even back in college, he always had a dozen bowling pins in the air: you seldom had his undivided attention. It was annoying at first, but one came to accept that this was just Everett, the Renaissance man, some kind of prodigy who seemed capable of being many people at once. In matters great and small, he had helped Laird, but on other occasions – when his old friend seemed bedeviled by some conundrum of his own –he became invisible, incognito. Everett was that sort of enigma — close to everyone and no one.

Laird recalled a mutual acquaintance logging their strange friend's travels after graduation: Manchuria, Yemen, Tierra Del Fuego and then on to New Guinea. He circled the globe, purportedly on some wild photography gig, though it was rumored that he'd been fired after two months and was merely racing through a trust fund.

Postcards alluded to decrepit ferries, tribal feuds, casbahs, all the daring escapades Laird never had the pluck to consider.

About five years before, Everett resurfaced, flogging some suspicious investments in Albuquerque. There were a few emails exchanged, usually when other alums started sounding off about a cherished old haunt on campus being demolished, or a scandal involving a member of the faculty. After a while, Everett's stint as a broker ran its course and he'd begun his own business, a consulting firm whose purpose was unclear. His missives tended to be cryptic, almost coded in their allusions, the bottom of them always embroidered with a quote from some distant figure no one had ever heard of: Albertus Magnus, Saint Jerome, Obato Kindu, Al Farabi, Dangmar Blintz.

One afternoon after lunch, Laird found a note pressed beneath the crack in his office door. It was on stationery whose design showed two men standing back to back at a fork in the road – the signs on each post composed in some arcane language. Their indecision was palpable. The quote beneath was some Icelandic proverb that read, "How can one be honest, when the deep truth is often so obscure?" Inside was Everett's large haphazard script explaining that he had flown in for a project, and that they should get together.

He suggested a bar called "Parallel" that was not too far up Water Street in the tiny Bogenville district. Laird wasn't sure what motif this represented, but the walls were covered with different images—soldiers, planes, trains, Romans, cats—all moving in close ranks that didn't intersect. Laird thought that this lack of apparent meaning, and the room's slight vertiginous cast, must have been part of the place's allure.

Glimpsing Everett at a table in the back, Laird thought he looked changed though it was hard to say how: a few lines here or there, the scruffy beard gone. Yet still there was that almost gaunt thinness, unruly hair, craggy nose, that same rakish profile and air of being lost in a trance. He was moving the salt and pepper shakers around in different positions as if they were pieces in a board game.

"So you still exist. Amelia Earhart would be easier to track down," Laird said, unable to restrain a broad grin. He remembered at least three occasions where he had tried to contact Everett in vain—his location having changed without notice.

"Yes, well, there's always something on the other side of the mountain."

"I'll have to take your word for it." Laird winced, thinking of his own provincialism, and tried to flag down a waitress who was busy navigating the narrow spaces between tables. He would need a drink to help solve the riddle of his old companion.

"You look terrific. Most people are probably better off staying put," Everett said, staring with that odd intensity.

Laird wondered if this was a subtle dig and couldn't help but kid Everett about his transience. "For a while there you must have been renting month to month. You took up half my address book."

He remembered one of Everett's infamous shacks just after college, where the floor was tilted so much it was more like a ramp. He cut down the legs of the furniture on the high end so it all somehow looked level. The joke was that it was perfect for dates because the bed was in the lowest corner so at least he had gravity on his side. Laird also recalled a long wood flute which emitted a low, mournful sound that might have been a precursor to his bizarre exploits.

"By the hour," Everett said in a tone that managed to be both self-deprecating and mischievous. "Don't worry. It wasn't a bank robber kind of deal." He furtively glanced down at some electronic device half hidden in his pocket, but in a second he was back, peering at Laird with those peculiarly bulging eyes. He had once confided a medical name for this syndrome, but Laird had forgotten it.

"Don't worry," Laird responded, beginning to feel the salutary effects of his gin and tonic. "Whatever it was, the statute of limitations has probably run out."

They swept through a preliminary discourse of their general circumstances. For Laird, this consisted of three marvelous kids, his drone position with Trident Cellular, the carriage house in tranquil Hedgewick. He would have liked to unburden himself about the madcap nature of his domestic life, the impossible juggling act, but he had enough social acumen to withhold all that. As usual, Everett seemed a bit coy about his side of the story, yet Laird managed to extract that he had made a small killing on a titanium mining stock and decided to get out. "Before the gods of finance turned on me," as he put it.

He didn't seem any more eager to talk about his current enterprise. "It's a service kind of thing," he said, rearranging the silverware. "A little difficult to explain."

"It must be great being your own boss," Laird said, picturing his own: a short, stout man who managed to be both well-meaning and borderline psychotic.

"Of course, but you have to be willing to accept the possibility that the whole thing could blow up at any minute," Everett confided, with a look of mock embarrassment. He illustrated his point with a close call he'd had in Kuala Lampur when a remote colony of Malays once forced him to flee in a rusty jeep due to an error in translation. As he recounted this, Laird's restless classmate glanced at the odd designs around the room, as if attempting to penetrate their secret.

"What in God's name is it?" Laird blurted, unable to suppress the question any longer. Finding out what Everett was up to now was a subject of great interest not only to him, but also to their small coterie from the old days.

"I'm in the excuse business and don't try to convince me it's some kind of menace to civilization. Quite the contrary." He reached into his wallet and pulled out a card – the logo, the same Janus image Laird had seen on the previous note. This time, the figures appeared like they were about to pace off a duel, though the pistols were nowhere in evidence. The sketch was situated over the words "Perfect Excuse, LLC."

Everett launched into a diatribe about how the earth would fall off its axis without a necessary degree of fabrication. It was an interpersonal lubricant, a means of avoiding conflict at every turn. "It's not like I'm inventing deceit here. Statistics show that people shade the truth on average nine, ten times a day. The main thing is that it's often done poorly which can result in anything from mildly wounded feelings, to complete mayhem. That's where I come in."

"But Everett, let's face it, wouldn't it be better if people were simply more direct?" Laird argued, trying to keep his voice down beneath the mellow piano riff playing in the background.

"That's like saying, wouldn't it be nice if all the men were handsome and all the ladies ravishing?" he said, a rapid succession of blinks marking a rare display of irritation. "Now I grant you that deflecting guilt isn't the best course in all instances, and I unequivocally tell my clients that. There are plenty of cases I refuse right off the bat. I won't do child support, or phony sales, or outright jilting at the altar. Naturally, I won't do anything when a crime's been committed. Let the lawyers handle that."

As he went on, Everett became more vehement that the endeavor be seen in an altruistic light. Everyone disastrously messed up at one time or the other, yet this could usually be healed if one got past the initial shockwave– the emotional blast – the sense that every assumption has been false. Some "temporary subterfuge" was necessary to restore an atmosphere where rational dialogue could take place again. Despite the fact that the whole idea sounded absurd, Everett had done a great deal of research on pretexts, alibis, every sort of linguistic maneuver, until they had been honed into a kind of magic. A perfect excuse wouldn't be your standard amateur falsehood, riddled with transparent inconsistencies: it would be a masterpiece of illusion.

"I can't say I altogether approve, but I must admit, the whole concept has the signature of your diabolical brilliance," Laird said, as they clinked glasses. Everett allowed a small, inscrutable smile.

"Well, it's a living," he said. "I wish I could stay but I have a client at two. Opal, an interesting challenge."

"Tell me more," Laird demanded, raising his eyebrows.

Everett released a faint sigh and clasped his hands together like a vice. "You don't want to know."

As the party approached, Laird recalled many such celebrations for the older kids, and imagined this one would be no different. The combination of both sides of the family created a malevolent influence that rendered him a caricature. It would take form in the half hidden corners of a smirk, and long stretches of conversation where he seemed to be ignored. Certain embarrassments were bound to drift up to the surface like dropped cargo in a shipping lane. Someone might mention how Laird had hit the wrong button on the disk player triggering French subtitles to scroll across the bottom of the screen for weeks. Uncle Charlie would point out that Laird's vote in the last election had sent the country into a death spiral.

He would lay ten to one odds that the broken Turkish hotplate would come up. Hannah had purchased the antique at an estate sale and it had been wrought with such vibrant hues that they exhibited it on the kitchen cupboard. One weekend, he had bumbled through the swinging door juggling three grocery bags, startling their dachshund, Caesar. Laird tripped,, hurling a head of lettuce into the plate as the dog scrambled to his feet. Its azure arabesques shattering beyond recognition. They would all laugh when Hannah recounted

Laird's defense that Caesar shouldn't have been laying by the door; he was being "tried and sentenced without a jury." Now he wondered if Everett's service might have helped him shift the blame, advised him to put a big chunk of the dish in Caesar's mouth just before Hannah got home, or produced some fraudulent seismograph to show there had been a small tremor at the instant of the mishap.

Ten days before the festivities, Laird got a call from Jim Ogden, a highschool buddy who had moved to the East coast a few years before. After a pleasant conversation harkening back to their robust youth, Jim told him he had two tickets to the US Open he'd won in a charity raffle. They were in the 17th row – aisle six – merely a fraction from the ideal center court view. The way the brackets were set up, the tournament was likely to feature a rematch of Nadal vs. Federer, titans of the modern age, making history one way or the other.

When Laird and Jim had been on the tennis team together, they would muse about Flushing Meadows, the splendor of the grounds, the roar that would explode from the rafters when a player made a diving volley. Tickets for the finals were as rare as Leatherback turtles, unless you were Jack Nicholson or the Prince of Wales:Laird said yes before he even checked the calendar. With the late flight, he could make it a one-day trip. When he hung up the phone, he felt the kind of thrill he hadn't had in a long time; that the world was again full of unseen possibilities.

After an endless meeting, as he began to flesh out the details, he realized that the excursion and Nell's party inextricably collided. There was an agonizing moment when he felt as if he were being split in half, drawn by diametrically opposed forces of nature. He knew Hannah would never accept his failure to appear. Her own father had been of the intermittent variety and this hole in her familial past was the wellspring of all her disappointments. She would have won the essay prize, the coveted role of Desdemona in summer stock, the trip to the Greek Islands for selling the most girl scout cookies—fill in the blank—"if only he had been there, really there."

Laird briefly thought about how he might finesse the whole thing but here was the stuff that accumulated like bad karma, which careened toward divorce. It was easy to imagine Hannah's attorney asking Laird's whereabouts when the candles were puffed out atop the swirls of frosting. The word unforgivable would scroll across the judge's mind like a Times Square marquee when it was revealed that his absence, far from being due to some unforeseeable glitch, was as rigorously planned as a state funeral. Laird brooded over the call he would have to make, how he hated ever to break a pledge, especially when Jim had chosen him over a score of others who would jump at the chance.

He had a dentist appointment for a broken crown that would at least give him a couple hours to consider how to break the news. In the office, he picked up an eight month old Newsweek, and came upon an article whose front section depicted an idyllic scene with the title "Proof of Heaven?" about a woman who was convinced she'd been whisked to a sort of paradise during cardiac arrest. Once Laird settled into the chair, Dr. Henzell was not surprised to hear that the tooth had broken while his patient chewed a piece of wheat toast. "That's the way it is. Soup, mashed potatoes. The straw that broke the camel's back."

Laird elected to get gas for all the drilling it would take to file down the cracked tooth. Thirty seconds under the mask, and he somehow began conflating heaven with the US Open: the pop of the ball off the rackets, the geometric beauty of the net held taut and expectant at the poles, all the calculated and graceful movement. A few of the comments Everett had made arose like the captions on his misfiring TV – how truth, at least as an absolute principle, was highly overrated. Everyone had his own slant and the need for nuance, even outright chicanery was practically universal. Before he staggered out of the office, he had somehow become convinced that he needed Everett's assistance.

They met at Everett's apartment which had the atmosphere of a museum no one would ever be foolish enough to visit. It contained a rhinoceros tusk, the kind of basket a cobra might slither out of, erotic wood carvings, a fuzzy crystal ball. Laird recalled how in the early days Everett would affect a weird style of dress that involved a string of beads hanging from his belt, or a hat festooned with some rare feather. Though such quirks repelled many, Laird supposed he'd been fascinated by the sheer audacity of the man. His own inherent sense of propriety was like a dominant gene, and he couldn't help but admire the brazenness with which Everett seemed to defy every convention.

"Remember, you're replacing one reality for another if you want to succeed. It has to be just as solid, maybe even more tangible than what actually occurred," Everett counseled with that mixture of assurance and distraction Laird had never quite come across in anyone else. The process required corroboration, "secondaries" that were witnesses, or other supporting evidence to make the excuse seem incontrovertibly true. Of course, Laird had vast reserves of skepticism for anything so dubious, but it was hard to fault his mentor's logic at any point. The system seemed nearly foolproof.

"You could always tell her the tennis thing is a fait accompli and go on offense, but I wouldn't recommend it," Everett explained. "This is where you rack your brain for some meaningless mistake on Hannah's part. Forgetting to pick you up at the train station. Throwing out an old Beatles album cover now worth a couple hundred bucks; donating a pair of tarnished cufflinks, which turn out to be an heirloom from your great granddad who was killed in the Ardennes in 1918. Those tit for tat arguments usually don't end well." Everett closed his eyes and shook his head rapidly just picturing the rancor.

"I agree but what am I going to say? Hannah trusts me, but she isn't blind."

"Of course not. There's a whole different set of hoaxes for the blind... I'm kidding." Everett threw up his hands for a second like a prisoner surrendering. "I don't think we should go with a physical injury. There's the limp and the winging scapula, but you'd have to keep that up for a month. I'd say your situation calls for the 'series of delays' paradigm. Here, see which one of these seems the most practical."

Everett picked up a gigantic book whose cover was embroidered with a sinuous gold pattern, as if he were presenting a sacred tablet. It contained a catalog of richly detailed scenarios with an appendix to help choose them.

"It goes without saying that the delivery is crucial: the more outlandish the excuse, the more essential that it be uttered with absolute conviction. You cannot flinch or permit any doubts. You have to be so familiar with every iota of the story that you damn near believe it yourself. Remember, you're not just helping yourself. You're helping Hannah too."

"How am I doing that?" In twelve years, Laird could count on one hand the number of times he'd fibbed to Hannah, always over some trifling matter like how many steps he'd climbed at the gym.

"You're protecting her from seeing the real you," Everett said, his arms akimbo like the finale of an opera. "Believe me, if everything were completely transparent, we'd have Armageddon."

"Alright, this might work with some tweaking," Laird said, as he perused the options, his discomfort overcome by necessity. "Let's say there's another dentist appointment that morning. Henzell could spot something on an X-ray. It's all rush, rush to the hospital. My phone's battery goes dead. They won't let me leave without a release.

There's some kind of traffic jam of emergencies. I'll email her that it's just standard procedure – a silly precaution you have to go through."

"I swear you've got a knack for this. We'll have to find out how far it is from the dentist to the hospital, the names of a few doctors, and get the fake documents. Say Henzell was on vacation and set you up with someone else Hannah won't be familiar with. Some name impossible to spell. You'll need a secondary, but there's no time to line that up so I'll have to do it." Everett had picked up a four foot long gourd, which may also have served as a type of horn, and peered straight down into its gap as if looking for a djinn. Then he got a call, the ring tone a cacophony of seemingly prehistoric instruments, and held up an index finger to signal this wouldn't take long.

"Please don't do that Opal," Everett said, turning away, caught in an uncharacteristically vulnerable pose. He had let it slip that she was his most important client, and that she needed more ruses in a month than most required in a lifetime. There was even the barest hint – no more than the flutter of intuition – that he had fallen in love with her, despite the risk of such a development. "Just wait for me," Everett said, almost burying his head in the receiver. "I can be there in a half hour." Laird hated to infringe on anyone's privacy so he waved goodbye, and left $200 in cash on a bureau populated by several crude paintings of witchdoctors.

The sun shimmered on the tournament grounds, the precise rectangular spaces radiating an aura of transcendence. There was just enough of an eddying wind to offset the heat. Jim greeted Laird with a bear hug, and after they grabbed a couple beers and meandered to their seats, the iconic scoreboard looming above, they reveled in the alternating hubbub and silence that surrounded the contest. The acrobatic display of the match, the phenomenal speed, the rhythmic chords of balls compressed against the strings were all mesmerizing. It was not until the fourth set that Laird's qualms crept in, lightly at first and then like a torrent. He began to miss key points, not react to the infinitesimally close calls and swoons of the audience. When Nadal won a crucial tiebreaker and everyone else leapt up, he realized that for some interval he had not registered a thing.

Laird was playing out the scene of his return for the hundredth time. It was like one of those Star Trek episodes where the transporter has Captain Kirk stuck in limbo between point of origin and destination – neither here nor there. He had already emailed Hannah a vague account of his phony whereabouts so she wouldn't alert the National Guard. Everett would text him just before he walked up the flagstones to the entrance and call him five minutes after he arrived, as "Dr. Solomon" to confirm everything was just fine.

It had been dark for hours when Laird arrived, a piece of gauze with red dye fixed inside his cheek. He fumbled briefly with the lock and once inside permitted himself to survey the chaotic aftermath of the revelry. Cone hats and tiaras remained scattered across the couch. Balloons clung to the ceiling and cake crumbs were still piled like miniature dunes across the ribboned table. A glittery message of congratulation had started to peel away from the far wall. The kids must have already gone asleep because the only sound was from some sitcom, probably one of the comedies Hannah liked, in the den. He felt guilty, yes, but also as ready to do his act as a Broadway veteran on closing night. Even before he saw her across the dimly lit room, Laird launched into his apology, laden with distress, lamenting the obstacle course he'd encountered.

"Laird?" Hannah cried, edging out into the hallway. She was wearing a sweatshirt that had a smear of chocolate ice cream trailing across it like a comet. Her face was an amalgam of rage, sorrow, doubt and fear of the unknown. He nervously stuck his hand in his front pocket, and discovered the stubs from the match and the train that he had neglected to destroy. There was a terrifying second when his wife's very presence, coupled with evidence of his betrayal, seemed to cause a short in his brain. But Everett had made Laird swear he would go through with the plan and instilled a certainty that faltering in the middle would only lead to shame and heartbreak.

"I'm so sorry, honey," Laird said delicately, making sure to meet her eyes, the script kicking in. The delivery did not go exactly as rehearsed days before in the decrepit tool shed next to the alley, but at least he was "committing to the role," the phrase Everett so often used. Hannah was studying him, suspended between the volcanic agitation of disappointment, and a tender anguish that something might really be wrong.

"Are you alright?"

"Fine. I'm sure it was just a formality. They said..."

Laird's phone began to ring, too early, throwing off his rhythm but he managed to stammer "this might be the doctor" as Hannah sat down with her legs under her on the chaise lounge. Next to Laird's ear, the device felt as charged as a hand grenade. Everett's voice came through the receiver with too much volume, with a reverberating edge of turmoil, so Laird took a couple steps away toward the window.

"You can't imagine how Opal has turned the tables, Laird. With her, it just isn't a fair fight." He said this with the unmistakable slur of intoxication, and Laird recalled some snags Everett warned could rattle the performance, but this wasn't one of them. Laird nodded his head a few times as Hannah, unable to hear a thing, remained riveted to every adjustment of his expression.

"That's great to hear Dr. Solomon," he said, smiling uncertainly, wary of lapsing into melodrama. "I can't tell you how grateful I am you would let me know right away."

There was no trace of the fake repartee that they had put together. Everett kept rambling that he and Opal had to leave immediately for an island in the Azores where he would be incommunicado, but that Laird could always leave a message through Raul Montreaux, a spear fisherman nearby, if something came up. Laird instinctively knew that Everett's contact was nonexistent, that the phone number he'd rattled off had been chosen as randomly as a lottery sequence, but that was a predicament for another hour. Everett's emotional condition was deteriorating with each phrase such that he now seemed to be gasping for breath. "Don't worry, Laird," he added just before the connection went dead. "You're a natural. If anyone can be in two places at once, it's you."

"That's terrific," Laird replied into a void of static. "You do the same."

He turned to Hannah, a look of relief mingled with exhaustion etched across her lovely face, as if in a film close-up. For the rest, there would be a strong dose of regret to draw on—he would spend the entire next day doting on her and Nell—though he would not have undone his deed for all the tea in China. But the call had thrown him off somehow: the lines Laird had imprinted so indelibly began to blur. His concocted series of misfortunes kept fusing with the buzz in the crowd when Federer had lifted the glinting trophy over his head, until it all became as nebulous as a dream.

"So what happened?" Hannah pleaded, with all her poignant loveliness.

When Laird hesitated, Everett's face seemed to drift up in the guise of one of his shamans, with wild streaks of paint radiating across the room. Some other voice in Laird's head seemed to whisper that he could still turn back, confess the whole story and the love of his life would understand, reach out and forgive this wayward impulse as she had so many times before. Yet, beneath her searching gaze, he wavered, pitched back and forth by currents of memory, the truth so shadowed now with separate versions that he was unable to utter a sound.

September

Leanne Hoppe

A history making itself known
to the six-mile dirt road out.
Toadstools. Firewood from an empty hillside,
fossil grooves, three bucks,
foil potatoes cooked by flame light and headlight.

That wants to be proven wrong.
Sod house. As it's thought on returns:
the light, heat from the burner,
eastern snoring, too bright sunrise.
I am not thankful to have something left.

Winter Scene

Katherine Lazarus

Snarling fox, flustered
turkey, and a white hare
watching, unremarkable
in still, fresh snow. And
the other two, entwined in

hunger and hunger
for life. They flurry
snow into the air, unaware
of the staring hare,
leaving ruby feathers

on the foothill. Upon flesh,
teeth sharpen with death
as cool as the drifting
solstice air. And the hare
knows to press away.

Rain Again

Katherine Lazarus

For all the answers
you can't Google
I drove along
the road-split mountain

where I don't get
service
on purpose. I'm in love
with possibilities, serendipity—
a moment

without the infinite
phone connection.
Because I can't

remember what life feels like
without everything all the time,

and I got surprised by sweet rain
a kind of friend
down the window pane—
a shortcut home.

The Return

Mary D. Chaffee

I pause for a moment at the top of the hill. Below me, the road narrows to a rough dirt track winding down into shadow – the farmhouse unseen around the bend. About to descend, I'm gripped by sudden uncertainty. Although I've come so far to find answers, a part of me – the part I've learned to listen to – whispers that sometimes it's safer not to know.

Behind me lies the village, its few remaining residents going about their everyday affairs on this hazy August afternoon. It would be so easy to pull a U-turn, go back to Palen Sweets for a second cup of coffee while I mull my second thoughts.

I park my rented Prius in a patch of weeds by the roadside and get out. I take a deep breath, inhaling the scent of goldenrod and clover. It's time. I reach for my backpack, lock the Silver Bullet and start down the hill.

At the first bend the maples draw closer together, almost touching. For a moment the air chills and the hair stands up on the back of my neck. Ahead, all is cloaked in shadows despite the glow of the setting sun.

A touch of vertigo and I sway. Then it passes and I continue.

They say that home is where, when you go there, they have to take you in. But what if you arrive and the windows are dark and empty, the front door sagging on its hinges, the silence around it broken only by furtive rustlings under an acre of neglected apple trees?

Years have passed. But finally the pull of nostalgia has proved stronger than the undertow of memory. So you left on this journey, clinging to hope. Because, face it, you needed to see. To prove to yourself that everything was fine, had always been fine. That what you believed was real, was merely the product of the overheated imagination of a teenager who had read too many Lovecraft tales and smoked too much dope behind the barn, with Teddy. Big brother Ted, thirteen months older than you and, everyone agreed, so much wiser. The family had assigned roles to us early on. Teddy was the rational one, and you were the loose cannon – well, someone had to be.

When Teddy woke in the middle of the night to the sound of a faint, almost musical keening, he put it down to our dad's old transistor radio. He made heavy-handed jokes about it in the morning, not noticing that you'd gone quiet. Because when the nearly inaudible lamentation interrupted your uneasy dreams you'd covered your head with a pillow to deaden the sound. Still its vibration continued, a cry for help at once pitiful and malevolent.

Teddy must be pushing thirty now, but your mind's eye conjures him as he looked at seventeen: the last time you saw him. A ruddy round face framed by a thatch of dirty blond hair; a squat, strong body like our mom, and a pair of clever blue eyes that said I'm blowing this pop stand as soon as I can wangle a scholarship to a decent college. Teddy wanted to be a lawyer, for the money. You wonder now if he ever made it.

Your parents, stolid apple growers, were clueless. They didn't understand either of their kids, especially you. True, most teenage girls complain about the same thing. But Mom and Dad expected clever, lazy Teddy to take over the backbreaking orchard and cider-bottling business, and you, the disappointing one, to stay out of trouble until some unsuspecting sucker married you and got you pregnant, in that order.

The year you turned sixteen was filled with tension. Most days you skipped school and hung out in the woods, yearning for freedom. Why bother to attend classes? College was off the table for females in your family. Most nights you slept fitfully, tormented by nightmares. It was worse when you lay awake, aware of being targeted by malevolence, more terrifying because it was undefined. A door whispered shut, moved by no breeze. A picture frame jumped off the wall and shattered – you were blamed for that. The cloying scent of rotten fruit filled your night-shrouded room, then faded as quickly as it had appeared. And always, that mournful high keening. You could almost make out words, just at the edge of your hearing.

"Help...meeee..."

Finally, you couldn't take it any more. And so, after yet another sleepless night, another displeased, uncomprehending lecture from your mom, another unresolved argument with your dad, you ran away.

You would have been easy to find, if your parents had bothered to search. According to that last hurried phone conversation with Teddy, they had basically washed their hands of you. He wanted to know where you were calling from. You didn't tell him.

You were hiding in plain sight, in Manhattan. It could have been much worse. Sad but true: young girls arrive in the big city every day and are eaten alive – by drugs, pimps, disease, pregnancy. By rats.

Your story was different. Arriving like a refugee fleeing from a war zone, a refugee's urge to thrive by any means necessary reared its head. That first night was the low point – you dozed warily on a bench in Riverside Park with your backpack for a pillow, clutching a Swiss Army knife and checking and rechecking the meager store of crumpled tens and twenties stashed in an old stocking tied around your belly.

The next day you paid for coffee and a muffin, used the restroom to get clean, and hit the street running. At every 'help wanted' sign, you lied about your age, used a fake name, and to your vast surprise after four days had talked your way into a job bussing tables and cleaning toilets at a greasy spoon on the Lower East Side. Minimum wage but all you could eat, which helped, if you could choke the swill down. You took home just enough to cover week-to-week rent in a cockroach-infested broom closet. You were in heaven.

From there, the only way was up, and you took it. Online classes to get your GED, writing classes at The New School, a job that paid better, and another, better one after that. Human beings for roommates instead of a thousand roaches. Early on, you paid a small fortune for forged documents that made your new identity legit. Gone was Sabrina Joy McCann, truant, disobedient daughter, the loser haunted by imagined demons. In her place rose Amber Lockwood, a woman with a future. Sabrina Joy's unkempt mouse-brown locks were replaced by Amber's glossy auburn bob, just long enough to pull into a professional–looking bun. Braces straightened your crooked front teeth. Contact lenses turned your mud–colored irises turquoise. YMCA workouts slowly replaced fat with shapely muscle. Once, passing a mirror, you smiled at the image looking back at you, an intimate, feral smile that said, "Fuck 'em all!"

You grew comfortable with living a lie that felt more authentic than the truth you'd left behind. Thirteen years had passed since the waif morphed into warrior. Now you were a junior editor at Blade, a web-based fantasy and horror rag, a shoestring but edgy operation. They'd put you in charge of winnowing the slush pile. Blade paid enough to live on – just -- but it was a great place to make contacts in the business. You didn't intend to stay there long.

Most of the submissions that came in over the virtual transom were the usual drivel: dragons, elves, spells, demons, gore, the undead, portals to other dimensions. But one, a novella, caught your attention: the tale of a middle-aged sci-fi writer, struggling to finish his novel's final draft. It's overdue, his agent is after him, but he's stuck. Desperate, he rents an old house in Vermont, hoping that peace and quiet in the fresh air will cure his writer's block.

The house has other ideas.

As you reviewed the novella, your attention was drawn to the description of the old house, a farmhouse. You recognized its narrow rooms, the uneven flooring, the bedrooms papered with a faded pattern of cabbage roses, the stone-flagged patio with its mossy fringe. The kitchen's sour smell. The orchard heavy with unpicked Macouns and McIntoshes. The rough dirt road winding upward from its dead end just past the barn toward the village a mile away. All so realistically drawn. So familiar.

Blade rejected the novella in spite of your enthusiastic recommendation, but you took the manuscript printout home. It was a touchstone of sorts. A fiction had carried you far from your severed roots. Could fiction be drawing you back?

At first you resisted. But after the dreams began, vivid encounters with your family featuring the prodigal daughter's return to love and admiration, you began to see how it all might be possible.

Before me the ancient farmhouse looms. The windows are dark

and empty, the front door sagging on its hinges, the silence around it broken only by furtive rustlings under the acre of neglected apple trees. All is cloaked in shadows despite the glow of the setting sun. As the sun drops lower the colors of house and barn fade to the sepia tones of an old-time movie. It all looks strange, insubstantial. I shake my head to clear the cobwebs and walk closer.

The door creaks open and a young girl comes out. She looks familiar. Where have I seen that sallow face with its petulant expression, that body bulging from Levi cut-off, that threadbare Backstreet Boys tee shirt so like the one I used to wear?

Her lips twist into a grimace, but she greets me pleasantly enough.

"Can I help you?"

My eyes search her features. "Excuse me, but... do I know you?"

She scoffs. "I don't think so. My name's Bri. Does that ring a bell?"

I'm puzzled, so I ask her about the McCanns, my family. The ones who disowned me, the ones I've come to reclaim. Does she know where they moved to after her folks bought the house?

"We've always lived here," she tells me with a trace of impatience. "My gran was born here," she says like I must be nuts not to know this. I begin to suspect she's lying or mentally disabled.

"When will your mother be back?"

"My mother? Not for a long time." She grins, revealing crooked teeth. "Maybe never. Or soon. Take your pick."

While I search for an answer to this, she switches gears.

"Would you like to come in? I could make you a peanut butter and banana sandwich while you wait. On raisin bread," she adds, looking at me from under unplucked brows.

What an odd girl. For a moment I hesitate. But it's getting dark, I'm travel-weary and hungry, and *how did she know?* peanut butter and banana on raisin toast is my go-to comfort food.

I sit in the badly-lit kitchen with its familiar sour smell and wolf down the food, feeling almost like I've come home. Bri watches me eat, expressionless.

"My mother might be a while. Would you like to take a little nap?"

A power nap sounds good. It's been a long day and it's not over yet. Just to put my head down for a few minutes would be marvelous. I'm not looking forward to hiking back up the dirt road in the dark to where I've left the rental car, then driving 20 miles beyond the village to the inn where I've booked a room.

Bri offers to show me upstairs, but I tell her I can find my own way. She shrugs and hands me a flashlight: the electricity is shut off until the wiring can be repaired. I don't need it. My feet remember the old familiar way to the crooked little room with its cabbage-rose wallpaper and its mildewed scent. My bedroom.

We're alone in this house, just Bri and me. But as I drift off, I seem to hear the rise and fall of other voices, muffled by distance. No words, just gruff tones interrupted by shrill ones -- my parents arguing, always arguing. Always...

I awake in a void filled with darkness. I am alone, a speck of consciousness in a vast and pitiless place. Paralysis grips me. The dark is deep, final, permanent: an inky blackness like the spaces between the stars. I struggle, but it's no use.

And at last I'm able to cry out.

"Help...meeee..."

Somewhere, *somewhen*, a girl starts awake, terrified by the keening.

She can't take it anymore.

She'll be leaving soon.

Epistolary

Malisa Garlieb

You always replied.

    Imagine choosing everything wrong
        on purpose

and having it work out.

    The mothy coat, midnight text
    asking for *Anna Karenina*
        aloud.

        You said you'd seen the world once
          as it really was. Opening the front door,

        morning still on its knees,

pulsation through everything.

To feel
that animate again.

Because a well can be covered   with green wood,

inner chasms
with charm and wit,

you always replied—   xo
                                    make a wish.

Sapphires for day;
                all night, the bread of poetry
                    baked in its oven.

My work, runny   watercolors
                                        and figurines.

As welcome   as flowers in May,

confounding as genesis,
                gravity.

You always replied,

                walking backwards
with a trick   twitched hip.

Vertical drop into time:

Mother Mary appearing,   vesture of stars.
Masks of the feminine,   roses on a cross.

A decision once made has already been enacted.

You're the only other person I've
come upon.

Do you have a candle?

Trace

Malisa Garlieb

Other widows
keep plastic bags of dirty clothing.
An effort to preserve a scent

more distinct and loved than any bloom.

I've searched for yours
in your robe,
pillows,
the sweater you wore

before—
before—

You collected hats, coats, books, stones
(your daughter thinks you collected loves)
but I stashed gestures.

I can scroll through thousands
of smiles and fall
asleep to a recorded brogue.

Your bedside mess is untouched
but the smell of your scalp,
the planet of your chest, and the fulcrum
of our longing

       have vanished.

You collapsed   dropped

          every whorled petal
     and took your scent
  with you.

The Peace Cranes of Nagasaki

Karen Kish

I trace a curved outline up, around, down the angular pink paper figures huddled inside the frame. My finger is just a glass width away from a nuclear bomb descendant's flock of peace cranes. In the shape of a heart. In the exhibition hall of Nagasaki's Atomic Bomb Museum. Just meters away from Fat Man's ground zero.

***

Those diminutive cranes bring me back to the American School of Warsaw thirteen years ago and gentle Japanese sophomore Kunio Hara. Our English class had read Elie Wiesel's autobiographical *Night*, and each student had chosen a passage to dramatize or analyze.

Kunio quietly opened his excerpt. "This section describes Juliek, a musician who played in the Auschwitz band 'welcoming' Jews to the extermination camp. Now Juliek and the author are on the 42-mile wintry Death March evacuating 60,000 half-dead prisoners from Auschwitz to Buchenwald. Wiesel is speaking. He is 15 years old. Just like I am 15 years old.

> *It was pitch dark. I could only hear the violin, and it was as though Juliek's soul were the bow. He was playing for his life. The whole of his life was gliding on the strings — his last hopes, his charred past, his extinguished future. He played as he would never play again.*
>
> *To this day, whenever I hear Beethoven played my eyes close and out of the dark rises the sad, pale face of my Polish friend, as he said farewell on his violin to an audience of dying men.*
>
> *When I awoke, in the daylight, I could see Juliek, opposite me, slumped over, dead. Near him lay his violin, smashed, trampled, a strange overwhelming little corpse (p. 90-91).*

The Nazis forbade any Jew to play Beethoven. But now I will play for you Juliek's Beethoven concerto from that night."

Violin lifted to chin, Kunio's mournfully gliding bow echoed, honoring Juliek's soul.

We were all transfixed. I will never forget that moment. Nor the next one.

Kunio rested his violin on a chair, bowed slightly, and opened his hand. Nestled inside was a tiny paper crane. His gaze scanned us as he reached in his pocket and proffered a flock of eight rainbow cranes, one for each of us.

As we each cradled a crane, Kunio finished. "Elie Weisel was liberated from Buchenwald, barely alive. That was the end of the book, but that wasn't the end of the war. Months later, the two atomic bombs in Hiroshima and Nagasaki immediately killed 150,000 people. The Japanese people ever since have only wanted peace, only wanted to end all nuclear weapons. For us, these cranes are an eternal symbol of peace."

Kunio bowed again as, weeping, we all stood to applaud him.

Kunio later told me the story of Sadako, a two-year-old Hiroshima survivor. Ten years later, she was diagnosed with leukemia, the so-called "A-bomb disease," and, adhering to Japanese legend that mystical cranes live for 1,000 years, she decided to fold 1,000 cranes so that the gods would grant her wish for life. She exceeded that goal, but died after eight months in the hospital. She is internationally immortalized in the book *A Thousand Cranes*. Kunio explained that Japanese organizations donate *senbazuru*, memorial origami chains of 1,000 cranes, around the world as a peace legacy for Sadako and all children who were victims of the atomic bombs.

That summer I ordered a *senbazuru* and shared those delicate cranes, and Kunio's story, with subsequent years of *Night* readers. One of those cranes, and Kunio's, still nest in my Warsaw journal.

***

Sandy and I study the battered, charred clock in the Atomic Bomb Museum.

"That's the time," I whisper. The brittle, twisted hands mark 11:02 on August 9, 1945. The exact time of Fat Man's detonation over Nagasaki.

The exact time, the exact place. Outside, at the ground zero monument, brilliant fronds of *senbazuru* cascade down the dark base of the tall Hypocenter Cenotaph with the translated inscription: "Let all the souls here rest in peace for humanity shall not repeat the evil."

Here I can actually touch the skeins of cranes, a tactile ripple gliding back 61 years.

Sandy paces the stone circles inlaid around the Cenotaph. "These circles are a frightening reminder of my Cold War duck-and-cover training."

I pause. I have a vague memory of those drills, but Sandy's remembrances are razor sharp.

He steps on the first circle, closest to the Cenotaph. "I was in sixth grade. Mrs. Firestone had a grudge against me because I was a disruptor."

His shoe grazes the stone arc. "So when it came time to illustrate bomb blast circles, she had a 'final solution' in mind for me. She pointed to a map. 'Ring one around New York City's Wall Street - complete destruction.'" Sandy moves to the next ring. "'Ring two, 30 miles to Darien, Connecticut, everything incinerated.'"

One more step to the third ring. "I couldn't help myself; petrified, I asked what about the next ring, our ring to South Norwalk. She looked straight at me with a dire grimace, and strode to the windows. 'Everybody in these two rows would be shredded with glass. And Sandy, since you interrupted my lecture, please change your desk to this empty seat next to the window.' A collective gasp of horror stalked me to my impending death."

I shake my head in disbelief. "What a spiteful teacher to scare you like that!"

Sandy shrugs. "Petrifying for an 11 year old. But realistic. Thirty years later, during my Project Harmony exchange to Petrozavodsk, Russia, a similarly ringed wall map eerily surrounded St. Petersburg in the Civil Defense classroom. A red thumbtack pierced the Petrozavodsk circle. A goggle-eyed gas mask glared at me on the teacher's desk. I realized then that they had been just as afraid of us as we were of them."

I don't have such emotional memories, but I do know what those circles meant in Nagasaki.

A lethal second best. The original target was Kokura, 100 miles away. But smoke from bombing raids obscured visibility, so the *Bock's Car* B-29 delivered the plutonium implosion device with a force two and a half times more powerful than Hiroshima's Little Boy to the industrial port of Nagasaki.

An air raid alert boomed at 7:48 a.m. and was canceled at 8:30. The next siren blared at 11:09, seven minutes *after* the blast.

Then those real-life circles. First, a blinding flash. Next a blistering inferno; spontaneous fires; blast-induced, hurricane-force winds.

Sandy's teacher, Mrs. Firestone, was right. Glass shards shredded, scorched skin melted, homes and factories imploded. Everything, everyone within a half mile of ground zero was pulverized. Varying death and devastation radiated in dizzying circles for five miles. And 35,000 people died within the first 24 hours.

* * *

Sandy and I tread gingerly across the lush gardens to a deep trench and glassed-in cross-section of soil strata. Sandy reads the nearby panel.

"This shows the composition levels of the city at the time of the blast and the layer of earth added over them later for radiation protection." He lowers into the opening.

I can't go down. *Radiation protection? Some dirt?* I scan the sun-splashed few hundred yards to the edge of the city. How can everything be so green, so verdant? How can this bustling metropolis be *right there*, so close to ground zero? What about the effects of radiation—where I'm standing, where they're living?

Another Warsaw image haunts me. Just barely after the fall of communism, we foraged for food at two understocked groceries and at *Sadyba*, an open market of listing tents and scrap-wood kiosks. Every time I paced the muddy alleys, an inner voice from school security echoed over and over: *Don't ever buy vegetables from a Russian. They're grown in Chernobyl.* A babushka with a Russian accent was always there hawking mushrooms. Radioactive mushrooms? I shuddered as I quickly passed by.

Scientists estimate that Chernobyl won't be safely arable and habitable for hundreds of years, and the Exclusion Zone's rings radiate for 1,000 square miles. Entire villages had to be bulldozed and buried. And yet, here Nagasaki is right *there*.

Sandy emerges from the trench. "There's a meter of protective topsoil over the entire blast area."

"And over how much of the five-mile radius?" I wonder aloud. "How much protection is one meter?"

It's Sandy's turn to gaze questioningly at nearby Nagasaki.

***

The 30-foot high Nagasaki Peace Statue looms above us; below it, a wispy breeze unsettles *senbazuru*. The man is seated in a semi-lotus position atop a black vault that contains the names of the August 9 atomic bomb victims and those who died of the effects of radiation in subsequent years. His dramatic pose, right arm swept skyward, the left extended toward the city, and grieving expression, are explained in the poem embossed on the base.It was written by sculptor Seibo Kitamura, a Nagasaki native.

...The right hand points to the atomic bomb,
the left hand points to peace,
and the face prays deeply for the victims of war...

Sandy and I turn around. A brick-lined path leads away to the Peace Fountain. Bursts of mournful, life-saving water frame a black stone plaque carved with the words of nine-year-old Sachiko Yamaguchi, who fatally drank from an oil-slick surface: "I was thirsty beyond endurance." A flock of water bottles symbolically placed by visiting pilgrims lines the base. Around them echo the anguished voices. "*Mizu! Mizu!*" Water! Water!

At the bus stop I break our respectful silence. "We still don't have answers. Ground zero is right there across this street. They started rebuilding *immediately*. There must have been radioactive fallout everywhere."

Historian Sandy explains. "Yes. But they didn't know that. This was a new weapon with no history, no known effects. Radiation is invisible, especially if you don't even know what it is."

I angle my view back toward ground zero. I can still see the fountain's too late, thirst-quenching plumes from here.

Sandy flourishes his tourist transportation pass. Our bus is here.

***

As I write this, 2020 marked the 75th anniversary of the bombings of Hiroshima and Nagasaki. In both cities many of the *hibakusha*, A-bomb survivors, have endured a lifetime of disfigurement, debilitating health, and cancers.

As I write this, the virtual Doomsday Clock rests at 100 seconds before midnight, 100 seconds away from man-made global annihilation. The farthest-away minute hand had been marked 17 minutes before midnight in 1991, after the Cold War ended. A shadow of Nagasaki's scorched clock ruthlessly tracks this poised minute hand. Today, 100 seconds is the closest-ever calibration to apocalypse as the world's nuclear arsenal now exceeds a cataclysmic 13,400.

As I write this, my company is a tiny peace-white paper crane, wings lofted, proud head high. It reminds me of gentle Kunio, my American School of Warsaw student, now a University of South Carolina associate professor of music history—with a specialty in music of postwar Japan.

But this fledgling was innocently folded by my grandson Benjamin. Diminutive wings spread, it seems about to take flight. Or to give flight for a full life for Benjamin, the full life that Sadako was denied.

Sadako died at age 12—the same age as Benjamin when I saw him last summer.

Those dizzying concentric circles have swirled over me ever since duck-and-cover elementary school: in post-Chernobyl, Warsaw,

Nagasaki, Benjamin's delicate crane. Today, those global radioactive whorls stalk all of us.

And yet, I make a fervently naïve wish for these papery lofted wings: take flight, a soaring emissary in an ever-widening diplomatic arc—as we listen, listen...carefully...to the *hibakusha's* pleas for peace.

The Clock is still ticking.

And that wolves whisper

Isabelle Edgar

You knew few things. That I woke up that morning
in a pool of my own blood and had to clean myself in the woods.

It rained that whole night, you trying to kiss ripples
into the pool in my collarbone. My inner thighs muddied by Cascade leaves
that I, squatting in ferns, tried to clean the blood with.
Cascade leaves stained with me.

You told me you'd lick it clean like the wolves we saw
in Michigan the year I turned twenty and I pushed your head away
into the passenger window, brushing the bridge of your nose.

And that driving to Lookout Mountain through grandfather moss
honeyed with the same mess morning made on me,
I knotted my limbs to each other, clove hitch, bowline,
slip. Termite trails are beautiful, you said, here, an orb spider,

and a lichen mustache and that wolves whisper while coyotes seduce
sound.

And that day, in Marblemount on the Skagit,
after so many days alone, I cried into your mouth,
a pool beneath your tongue.

hey honey or something

Isabelle Edgar

In between two tall mountains there's a place they call lonesome
Don't see why they call it lonesome. -Connie Converse

Your hands feel like dried apricots was the first thing you said to me
and from then on I started taking shorter baths.

The days that I don't feel like leaving silently are extraordinary.
Ringing in blush tones. You always look at me way too long. I miss
many things I said, and you said you wish you could be everything
that I miss: you are cans of sardines and broken glass, Japanese
maple, bay leaves, an eighteen year addiction to redefining respect.

I don't dry my hair– I don't have the patience. Instead I ring
the strands out on my wooden fire escape: quintessential chicago
architecture. A quick cavity sort of city. A I am never going to feel
anything fully sort of city. Pick your poison and stick to it. Can't be
a martyr and a saint. But you, you here, kiss my eyelashes and my
clothes fall off.

I brush crumbs onto the floor. I give up on puzzles. No one actually likes monogamy, you said and I decided to build something out of wood.

This, here, is full of superficial adulation, sticky slivers of grins. Overly positive people scare me. Please leave me alone which means stay right here quietly.

I can be alone with you because you're lonely too. So stunning. When we dance we don't touch.

In this little life we have a painting Lucca gave me when he decided he wanted to open a gallery. You said it looks like a finger painting and I got mad and said it looks like a woman. So far his gallery is just pile after pile of commissioned dog portraits because that's where the rent is at.

We got pierogis and the orange beer with the bee on it or the honey kölsch as you say and I learned how to spell kölsch. And I wore my nice coat, that dark lipstick from Ohio because you said we were going out to the kind of dinner where you worry you're gonna stain everything involved.

We went to that Polish restaurant. Got one of those grocery bags. With one of those scary smiley faces on it and went to sit in the snow. We didn't talk, my plum lip staining the plastic spoon.

When I'm on my way I'll keep my feet nice and quiet for you. Talking sweet to my dusty eyes, you'd like to hear it too.

I like your shirt with the bear playing bass on it. Thread bare. I think I'm often a different type of temperature. You used to follow me outside when inside was full of people and their bad breath, buckling your knees over and over.

I told you about the half combed hair. I'm not so good at yelling when I should but I am good at card castles. Not houses of cards, the whole castle. You put the orange beer on top and it stays standing.

Off to two tall mountains. Maybe find Connie Converse in her underwater Volkswagen Beetle. So stunning, honey.

Just keep adding more vinegar and salt until it tastes good. Or lemon. I want to be very near to you, mycologist wannabe. Growing faster after lightning storms.

To be a red door, a rug. To be this tall without you. We built a bench together that neither of us will sit on. When we dance we don't touch. Fill our palms with fresh apricots. One of these days, someday, I'll exhale for you, clear waters.

Tabernacle

Charles Lewis Radke

habitation; esp., the human body conceived of as the temporary abode of the soul. *Webster's Collegiate Dictionary, Fifth Ed.*, 1939

MY MOTHER HAS SOLD THE HOUSE and informed me that she is moving into a trailer. She calls it a "mobile estate," and it is near the highway and a municipal park. There's a little creek running behind it where Styrofoam gets hung up in the reeds. On a Saturday afternoon, my mother calls and says she needs me to come claim the things I want. This will happen on Sunday, before supper, and then she wants us to stay and eat a last meal there. Me and my wife, Nancy.

"There are things here I can't take with me," she says. "I want them to go to *family*." She says to bring my own boxes. She packed everything she needs for the rest of her life, all of which will fit nicely into her trailer. She has it all planned out, right down to the bric-a-brac she wants in her coffin, which I have told her is also a mobile estate, when you think about it. She says she doesn't have time for my jokes. "This is no laughing matter," my mother says. "I want you to look through my things and make sure there's nothing you want."

"This is kind of strange, what you're doing," I say. "It is kind of strange that you are leaving a perfectly good house for a trailer."

"It is time for a change of scenery," she says, and hangs up.

I am sitting on the sofa next to Nancy trying to process all of this.

"You *know* what's behind it," Nancy says. This is one of those rhetorical questions she poses from time to time. Nancy knows that I know what's behind my mother's decision to sell a nice house and move into a trailer. It's our lack of children, that's what. This is my mother's way of punishing me, all because Nancy and I will not provide her with grandchildren.

Here's the thing: we are both into our forties now, and we have nice careers going. Nancy is a regional manager for a chain of fitness gyms, and I am in the insurance game: home-auto-life. I have my own building, even. It's in the Old Town section, right next to restaurants and antique stores. Once a month, my mother comes out to lunch before she goes antique shopping. I give her spending money just for that purpose. I can't do much more than that.

Nancy opens her mouth as though she is going to say something when my mother calls again.

"One more thing," my mother says. "You may want to bring Frank along for the organ." Frank is Nancy's first husband. He's a fit man, just turned forty, a few years younger than Nancy. He works at a factory that makes concrete pipes. Frank manages large infrastructure projects. He has rippling muscles, and whenever my mother needs something heavy carried from one place to another, she asks me to bring Frank, like he is a forklift and not a person. He also has a truck and a big heart to go with his muscles. He really is a sweet man, and very good-looking, like a movie star. My mother once said she couldn't understand what Nancy didn't see in Frank. It was like she was saying, "How could she choose *you* over *him*?" That was when I told my mother that Frank is gay. Turns out, this is what Nancy didn't see in Frank. Apparently, Frank didn't see it in himself until after he was married to Nancy. Now, he is married to a man named Henry, who is an engineer of some sort, so it's Frank and Hank, which has a nice ring to it. I told my mother this; she said, "Good for Frank!" My mother says that Frank is welcome to stay for supper too, and that he can bring Hank along, if he wants.

Nancy and Frank get along like two peas. It is really hard not to like Frank. This is not the case with my first wife, Judy, who was tough to love. Judy smoked pot, too much for my taste. I smoked a little here and there, but Judy smoked every night after work and didn't think I was very much fun to be around. She was always pressuring me to smoke pot and have some fun for a change. Those were her words to me almost every night: "Have some fun for a change," like I was a stick-in-the-mud, when all I wanted was to watch television and keep my wits about me. The fact that Judy couldn't be in my presence without being high should have been a big red flag.

After several years of being made to feel like a party pooper, I'd had enough. There were other issues–how could there not be?–but the pot smoking was the main one. Judy is now living in Colorado in a town called Pagosa Springs. She resides in a trailer with a guy named Tim. They snow-ski all winter, keep a bunch of dogs around, and get high together. Then in the summer they ride mountain bikes and run a grass-cutting business to support their dogs and their habits. This is a good life for Judy. It is the life she always wanted. When I told my mother what Judy was up to, she said, "Good for Judy!" like I was some terrible, un-fun burden Judy had finally gotten rid of.

The thing with my mother is that she roots for people like Frank and Judy because they are true to themselves. Those are the words my mother would use. In fact, those are the words my mother *actually did* use, back when she left my father. She said she needed to be true to herself, so she left him. And look where that got her: She never met anyone else. She wound up alone in a house, and soon she will be alone in a trailer, which is pretty much the bottom end of the lonesomeness scale.

Nancy says this whole thing is ironic. By choosing not to have children, Nancy and I are being true to ourselves, too, just like my mother once was. But instead of saying, "Good for you," my mother says we are being selfish. Nancy says selfish is what you are when your choices deprive others of happiness to which they feel entitled. Nancy is smart when it comes to figuring out people. I have told her before that she was a psychiatrist in her past life. I have told her she should be a psychiatrist in this life, too. She says she is just fine being an armchair shrink. Either way you slice it, Nancy has my mother down to a T.

I hang up after my mother reminds me about the organ. It is a pipe organ, about six feet by eight feet, which is small by pipe organ standards. If you set two tall refrigerators next to one another, that's about the size of it. The whole thing is inside a wooden cabinet, which my mother claims was in an English rectory more than a hundred years ago and played by a distant relative who was a viscount or something, maybe a duke. "We come from the British noble class," my mother has said before, but when you ask her for examples, she cannot come up with any. She says she'll look it up but she never does. That's why, with Christmas coming, Nancy and I are going to buy my mother one of those DNA ancestry kits so we can put an end to this once and for all. Still, though—no matter where it came from—we have the problem of the pipe organ. My mother has always assumed that it would be passed down from generation to generation.

Nancy hears my conversation with my mother. She is sitting

right next to me on the sofa, so how could she not? After I hang up, she says, "You will *not* bring that organ into this house, do you understand me? I don't care if it was played by the Queen of England."

"I am aware of how you feel about the organ," I say.

"That's good," Nancy says. "Because there needs to be no confusion on this one." It is at this point that Nancy gets up from the sofa and walks out of the room. This is how she plays it whenever she makes a pronouncement, like her word is the final one, and walking away is her version of the exclamation point. There is nothing left to be said on the matter. I see her disappear down our hallway; then I hear walk through our laundry room and into the garage. "I'm going to get boxes!" Nancy yells. What I hear next is the laundry room door slam behind Nancy. There. That is the exclamation point.

✕

IN THE EARLY YEARS OF MY MARRIAGE TO NANCY, my mother dropped all kinds of hints about children. She might offer Nancy a glass of wine or a cocktail when we were over, and then she'd say something like, "Unless you're *not* drinking *for some reason?*" She was hopeful that Nancy would say "As a matter of fact..." but she never did.

Nancy was good-natured about this at first. She'd respond with things like, "You never know," and she'd put two fingers over her lips and make herself blush, like Betty Boop. I have never known anyone who can make herself blush on demand, but Nancy sure can. I have quite a woman here.

This went on for a few years, throughout our late thirties, mostly. At the time, my mother thought her behavior was coy and cutesy. She said things like, "I'm going to have to put my knick-knacks up high when the grandbabies come." Or, "Do you know where I can get safety plugs for the sockets?" She said she was going to have Frank take out the recliner because she'd read that babies die in recliners all the time. "It's true," she told us. "Look it up."

She said things like this while we were in her house with her. She'd stand with her chubby fists on her broad hips like a crossing guard, then she'd touch her finger to the side of her face and screw up her lips and furrow her brow into a question mark. That was just the start and we tried not to think too much of it.

"She doesn't have anything else in her life," I told Nancy.

"That's one thing that needs to change, *pronto*," Nancy said.

Soon, Nancy grew to resent my mother's niggling. That's because her behavior grew less passive and more aggressive. She abandoned subtlety altogether. "I sure wish I had some grandbabies crawling around this house!" she'd say. This started happening after we turned forty. She started asking Nancy about her clock. One Sunday afternoon, my mother actually *ticked*. I mean, she went "*tick, tick, tick*," in front of Nancy, and when Nancy glared at her, my mother's eyebrows turned into little peaks on her forehead. "Are you guys gonna get busy, or what?" she said. Then she touched the face of her wristwatch with the tip of her pointer finger.

I thought this was uncalled for, and it was the last straw for Nancy. She said, "You talk with your mother or I am never going to visit her again." So I sat down with my mother one on one and let her know that Nancy and I were not having kids. I said, "Mom, we are too old." I said, "We cannot raise kids at our ages." We were at the Country Junction in Old Town, eating waffles and eggs. I said this was all my fault for choosing Judy at a young age. "I made a bad choice," I said. "And it's too late to go back and change it."

I paid the tab and we left, and I thought that was the end of it.

Still, my mother would not let it go. She called Nancy controlling. She accused Nancy of not wanting to lose her figure. "I mean, let's face it," my mother said. "It *is* her most valuable asset." Nancy does have a very nice figure. She is shapely, what used to be known as an hourglass figure. I think she looks like Marilyn Monroe sometimes. Anyway, my mother's comment about Nancy's figure irked me. It really got under my skin. Once again, we were at the Country Junction having a meal, and that's when I told my mother, "You're not being fair." I said, "Her figure has nothing to do with it. We are *just not having kids. Ever.*" I said this last bit a little louder so I could make my point. I needed to be emphatic on this one, and other diners in the restaurant turned and looked at us. It was that kind of moment where I drew my line in the sand. My mother cleared her throat then and dabbed at the corner of her mouth with a paper napkin.

"Ahem," she said. "I guess that puts me in my place then, doesn't it?"

She wouldn't look at me after that. Instead, she looked out the plate-glass window toward the street, which created this kind of dramatic effect as the sunshine glimmered in her tear-filled eyes. Her wattle trembled with her lower lip.

Imagine.

Then, this: "I don't suppose I have much left to live for then."

I said, "Mom, don't talk that way." I said, "You have plenty to live for."

Nancy and I had already talked about my mother living vicariously. Through us, I mean. She said my mother was relying on us for her own happiness and that she needed personal outlets. "She should join a seniors group at the church," Nancy said. "Or I can set her up with a free gym membership!" I suggested this to my mother, the thing about the free gym membership anyway, and she waved her hand at me like she was shooing a fly.

"What am I going to do at a gym?" she said. My mother is what you might call "heavyset," so the answer should have been fairly obvious. I mean, who couldn't stand to lose a few pounds?

"But there's swimming!" I said. "There's Zumba for seniors!"

My mother looked down in her lap. She folded her napkin into a square and tucked it away in her pocketbook. Then she stood up without finishing her lunch. "Put your Zumba where the sun don't shine," she said.

✖

FRANK AND HANK ARE MEASURING DIMENSIONS of the pipe organ while Nancy and I carry in empty boxes from the truck. My mother's boxes are taped and labeled in her scrawl. Bedroom. Bathroom. Kitchen. Living Room. Her trailer does not have a family room, she says, "so that's why there's no box labeled *family room.*"

Nancy rolls her eyes at this. I say, "Enough, Mother."

Frank and Hank glance at me with sheepish looks on their faces. Hank is not full of muscles like Frank. He is an engineer, after all, so he looks more studious, kind of wispy and delicate. His hairdo isn't as full as Frank's, either. He has a high forehead from his hairline receding. Nancy once called it a "fivehead" instead of a forehead, and I thought that was funny. I said, "Good one, Nan."

They are a good pair, Frank and Hank. I can see the whole brawn-brains dynamic, at least in my mother's living room. Hank is the brains of this operation. He established that the moment he walked into my mother's house. He clapped his hands together and said, "Let's take a look at this *behemoth.*" That was the word he used: *behemoth.* I could tell my mother found this insulting. Her nose pinched. "I can't watch," she said. She walked to the kitchen, where there was a chuck roast in the Crockpot and mashed potatoes in the oven.

"Something I said?" This was Hank talking.

I said, "Don't worry."

"There's no pleasing her," Nancy said.

Frank—sweet, muscular Frank—hollered after my mother. "Dinner smells lovely!" he said.

But there was no answer.

It was decided before we got here that the organ would make the trip to my mother's new trailer. This was after me and Frank and Hank paid a visit there. They took some measurements inside the trailer, along with the width of both doors: the front door on hinges and the back slider. Hank went around the trailer testing the stability of the floor with the toe of his boot. He pressed here and there to see if there was any give to the floor. Then he bounced up and down on both feet to see if the trailer rocked. He asked me and Frank to do it too, so all of us at once were bouncing up and down inside my mother's trailer to see if it rocked, which it did, but not enough to matter much, Hank said. Then he looked up to see how tall the ceiling was. There were these foam ceiling tiles that Hank pushed on; then he flashed a light behind them and saw some wires. He muttered "hmmm," and "uh huh," and "okay." He clicked his tongue inside his mouth.

All the while, there was the persistent sound of a measuring tape zipping and unzipping. Then Hank said, "I've got what I need," and we left.

Now, while Frank and Hank measure the pipe organ, Nancy and I pick through my mother's things. There are three bedrooms and two baths. There is a living room and a family room, what my mother calls a "den." We start there, where there is a roll-top desk that, I admit, would look kind of neat in my office in Old Town. It's one of those desks that a banker wearing a vest and visor would use while entering numbers into a ledger. The top door slides open with a wooden clatter, and inside there are lots of nifty slots for envelopes. It is some desk, I'm telling you. It really takes you back in time. Nancy agrees with me on the desk.

"I do like it," she says. "I think it will look sharp in your office."

She says it is an *accent piece*, and I tell her that's a good way to describe it.

"I might even use it," I say.

Nothing else really catches our eye in the den, or in any other room for that matter. Mostly, the furnishings in my mother's house are as old as the house itself. There is a sofa that sags in the middle, and that old recliner my mother thought would claim the lives of her grandchildren. There are small, scuffed end tables in the shape of hexagons, and golden lamps with fraying shades. There is an abalone shell in the center of a round oak coffee table. There is a fake tree with dusty leaves. We peek inside a closet to see a few shelves stacked with blocks and kids' board games. All new, all still wrapped in cellophane. That catches my eye, for sure, and for the first time during this whole thing, I get a pang of guilty sadness in my heart. Maybe it's the baby dolls, still in their boxes, looking back at me through black, glassy eyes. Nancy has noticed this too. We are both looking inside the closet at the things my mother has collected for the grandchildren she will never have. "This was our choice," she says. "This is what *we* wanted, remember?"

Nancy and I wander back into the kitchen. I am carrying a box with a few things as a gesture of politeness more than anything. There's a digital clock radio I can use in my garage to listen to ballgames. That's a good find. There's a framed cross-stitch my grandmother made of a French bistro, which Nancy says is kind of cute and crafty. There's a sleeve of unused light bulbs; some light, around-the-house tools; an aerosol can of wasp spray. We've got enough boxed up to feel like we've helped my mother unload some things.

We leave the box by the door. Meanwhile, the pipe organ is still in the front room as Frank and Hank look it over like a puzzle.

My mother is in the dining room forking chuck roast onto plates. She has stood a spoon in the dish of mashed potatoes. She also has a big bowl of green beans, warm dinner rolls, a jar of honey, and a soft stick of butter on a dish.

"Nancy, dear," my mother says. "Will you get ice for the glasses?"

"I can do that," Nancy says. "I can get ice for the glasses." She goes to the kitchen for an ice bucket and tongs.

"I'll tell you what," Hank says. He and Frank pull chairs up to the table while Nancy drops ice cubes into glasses. I follow behind with a water pitcher. "That's going to be some feat," Hank says. He casts a quick glance in the direction of the pipe organ.

"Thing must weigh about a thousand pounds," Frank says.

I give Hank a long, hard look. "Give or take," Hank says.

"Should we call the movers?" my mother asks. "Should we just call a company who specializes in moving pipe organs?"

My mother slops a heap of mashed potatoes on Hank's plate, right next to his pile of chuck roast. She does the same for Frank, then she follows that with some green beans.

"Looks delish," Hank says.

"Well?" my mother says. "Should we call a company?"

Hank says that with the right people, we won't need to call a company. "I think between me and Frank and the guys, we can get it moved for you," he says.

"We have tools and manpower at the plant," Frank says.

I'm eating my roast and not saying anything about it. What is there really to say on the matter? Frank and Hank have the whole thing figured, it seems, so all that's left for me to do is chew my food and drink my ice water, which I do, with some relish. Even for all my mother's shortcomings, she remains a terrific cook. She really knows her way around a kitchen. I'm feeling a mix of nostalgia and guilt as I eat my food and wipe my mouth on a cloth napkin. I say, "Mom, you really outdid yourself here."

Nancy says the same thing. So do Frank and Hank. Everyone at the table comments how wonderful the food is, how well-seasoned, how buttery and savory. Frank says it is a meal that sticks to your ribs, which is supposed to be a compliment, I think, but it sounds kind of snarky. My mother is sitting at the head of the table and she nods her head—in gratitude, I think—but she doesn't look at anyone. She nods and basks in the warm, complimentary nature of the moment. Then she blushes a little and goes back to eating.

✕

THE FOLLOWING WEEKEND, my mother calls to tell me she is settled in her trailer. "I'm feeling much better about everything," she says. "The grandkids, the move. I'm at peace," she says.

"I'm happy to hear that, Mother."

She says, "Just needed a change of scenery, like I said."

The trailer itself is narrow, but there's that little creek and that municipal park, which is much bigger than I imagined. Her back gate opens onto a walking trail where older people pad by with their dogs. This gives me an idea that instead of an ancestry DNA kit for Christmas, Nancy and I will get my mother a dog. The front door is on a cul-de-sac and yes, there is a highway close by and plenty of traffic noise, but all in all, I can see the attraction of the trailer. There appears to be a fair number of people in the mobile estate community that are my mother's age, and there is a sign when we drive in announcing Monday night Bingo in the rec hall. There is a schedule of events on an easel by the double doors and soon, according to the schedule, there will be a singer impersonating Neil Diamond. He goes by the name "Surreal Neil."

Nancy and I moved my mother's boxes on Wednesday after the Last Supper, after Frank and Hank and a crew of concrete pipe workers spent a couple of days installing the organ, which they accomplished after opening up an entire section of the trailer's side wall, like peeling back the lid of a sardine can. They brought in a massive hydraulic jack used on cement mixers, lifted the organ to floor level, and coaxed it inside. Then they zipped it up like surgeons. It was brilliant.

When Nancy and I visit that following weekend, I marvel at the scaffolding Hank put in beneath the floor. A subfloor, he called it, so strong it could support a Subaru or—in this case—a thousand-pound pipe organ.

Even though the trailer is bigger than I first thought, Nancy and I still feel wedged into the front room, where the organ stands like a monolith. It is taller than the inside ceiling panels allow, but Hank found a way around that, too, extending the cabinet into the interior roof space, then building a new ceiling around it. Now, my mother says, the sound carries straight from the organ through the metal roof to God. "I hope the neighbors don't mind," she says. "Already, I've seen some eyeballing the place."

"They just want to meet their new neighbor," I say.

"That's all it is," Nancy says. "They just want to meet you."

I have found a spot to stand in front of my mother's picture window. It's dusky. I have my hands in my pockets, looking over the cul-de-sac to the highway at the car lights zipping by. There is a low whooshing sound. It's kind of like hearing waves break on the shoreline, that kind of noise. Soothing, if I'm being honest, and what reason at this point should I not be? Nancy is sitting on the couch, flipping through pictures on her phone.

"What are you looking at?" my mother asks. She is standing in the living room behind me. I can't see her, but I can tell she is talking to me, not Nancy. Then, "What do you see out there, *Son?*"

And that's all it takes. I don't know why, but it's then—when she calls me *Son*—I feel a swell inside my heart I cannot explain. It buckles me. It's like someone punched me in the chest and I can feel my body recoil. My mother hasn't called me *Son* since I was a kid, but whenever she did, I felt like it made me part of something much bigger and more connected, the universe, maybe. That's it. I felt more connected to the universe as a son, and more sure of myself. There were people who came before me, you see, and I was building a life on their backs. Maybe that sounds corny and overstated, but that's what I felt anyway. Just tied to something bigger. "Son," my mother would say, "do you need some help with your algebra?" Or, "Son, can you ride to the market and get some milk?"

I am still standing in my mother's picture window, only now I can see her reflection move into the frame behind me. She is at the organ with her hands on her hips. The word "Son" slips from my mouth. "Son," I say it again. I say it so I can hear it now in my head, between my own ears. "Son, everything is okay," I say. "Son, you'll get 'em next time." I imagine myself speaking these words to someone other than myself. "Son, do the best you can."

I look in front of me and I look behind me. My mother bends to brush something from the bench before the organ, then she sits. It's crazy, but that swell in my chest begins to ache. It's like my heart is trapped inside a fist. I lean forward and rest my forehead against the cool window. I brace myself on the sill. "Honey?" Nancy says. "Honey, are you feeling okay? Say something."

"I'm fine, Nancy," I say. I take a deep breath and exhale. I breathe into the picture window and fog it up.

What else can I offer other than, "I'm fine"?

I press my hand flat to the glass. It feels cold, but the room is warm. My mother begins to play the pipe organ. The trailer at once fills with music, like something you'd hear in a cold church. I don't know who it is. If I had to guess, I'd say Handel, but that's because it's the only name that comes into my head. Whatever it is that my mother plays, it is so unexpectedly and hurtfully lovely that I can't speak. Outside, the sky darkens and lights begin to come on in other trailers. I see faces and figures shrouded in bathrobes. My mother's neighbors collect like penitents in the cul-de-sac, one after another, a crowd of the awestruck looking into the trailer for the source of this unspeakable beauty: this woman, this mother, this daughter, her fingertips, like feathers, floating up to the generous palms of God.

Out of the wind

Candelin Wahl

the sway and drone of white pines
a steady howl

a missing dog curls in a tree hollow
nose tucked under matted tail

inside a brick house, solid as
the smart piggy's

the wind keeps its owner
alert at three a.m.

she can't find sleep
her mind on smelly socks

sweatpants   his fleece blanket
laid out like prayer rugs

near the last known sighting
the edge of a fallow cornfield

anchored with stones
to foil the kick-up weather

snowstorm on the way

Mornings With Macky

Phoebe Paron

The sun predictably will show itself soon, until then
I turn on an artificial light
to illuminate our world.
I wonder what he thinks of the dark,
but I don't know how to ask.
Gentle noises, a small buzzing and occasional clinking
fills the kitchen. A once a day occurrence
to the usual sounds that accompany
being young and living with many others.
For now it is just us quiet creatures,
wordlessly mulling over our breakfast,
beginning the day with a shared meal,
me with my mush and him with his flakes.
Does he ever get tired of having this food?
I look over as he picks up a rock then spits it out.

Clink. I love our peaceful mornings.
I wonder what he thinks of our time together.
Do goldfish have thoughts?

Some Antics

John Kaufmann

By the time he ran into the Mexicans, Sammy had already lost his voice. This part of the country was what he had thought it would be like: dry, some scrub, flat-topped low hills. It was hot during the day, but cold and dry at night. It never rained. He kept up a chatter with himself, moving his lips and whispering for most of the time he spent alone. The sound of the chatter kept him company even though it was just a hiss in his mouth. He kept his eyes on the ground when he walked. That was a video of rocks, sand, pavement, grickle-grass, piping and, occasionally, blue sky to accompany the audio, but of course what he really saw were the people he spoke to. Guys from the school. Girls he had wanted to make jokes with. Witty retorts to things rides had said to him after they had left him off. His sleeping bag was canvas on the outside, nylon and feathers inside. It smelled like mildew and people. He would wake up alone on the ground, roll up the bag and eat something cold for breakfast. He rarely slept far from the freeway. On the way to the road, he would keep up his chatter. I could use a coffee. Cold this morning.

I love you. The shoulder was not designed for people. It was just blacktop, guardrail, asphalt. Beyond that – desert, scrub, low hills. Depending on where he was, the middle distance might have some buildings, pump jacks, power cables, a rail yard. It was always a rush when a car pulled over, like when a fish strikes. He would run up, open the back door, swing his pack onto the rear seat, dump himself into the front passenger seat, and exhale. If it was cold outside, the car would be warm. If it was hot, it would be cool. The seat and floor mat would be clean. There would be top forty or country, or, sometimes, Tejano music on the radio. He would usually fall asleep minutes after he sat down. While he was in a car, he was at home. Leaving felt like being ripped from the womb.

At night, he would wrap his right arm around his face, grab the nape of his neck with his hand, kiss his bicep, and say, "I love you". The hard ground crushed the feathers beneath him in his sleeping bag, but that no longer bothered him. Sometimes he would wake up shouting through his nose because his father was on top of him and strangling him, or the kids at the school were circling around him, rocking back and forth and jerking off.

He got tired of people asking him where he was from and where he was going. He would say, My father lost the farm, or My parents are dead. When he really wanted to be left alone, he would say, I'm a rattlesnake milker. When he said that his name was Sammy, people believed him. So, Sammy he became.

-How old are you?

- I'll be eighteen in a month.

-You have the world by the balls.

-*Hmph.*

He was terrified the first time it happened. A ride asked him where he was going. All he could do was squeak from the back of his throat. Where's that, the ride had said. *Squeak.* A tickle behind his uvula and a feeling of having lost a limb. When he reached around to grab his sign, he saw the ride flinch. He could not say, Relax. He windmilled the sign to the front and flashed the lettered surface toward the driver's seat: Tucumcari. Then he squeezed his right thumb and forefinger together and made a writing motion. *Do you have a pen?* The ride reached over to the glove compartment, bumping into his left knee with his knuckles. Here. He wrote on the corner of the sign, *Sorry.* The ride took off his baseball cap and smoothed his hair. You scared me, he said. Out the window, the desert slid by. Scrub, a few stunted trees, cliffs for a few miles then flatland, fast food joints, pawn shops, Automobile Alley, more cross streets, a few taller buildings. And then he was on the street, the waist-belt was biting into his hips, the sign was in a garbage can, the sun was overhead, and the ride was pulling away. To his right was a fake adobe building with a sign that read Citizens Bank. Across the street was a hardware store with a sign saying Trading Post and beside that Gutierrez Bail Bonding Co. Other than an old, dark-skinned wino sitting in a doorway, nobody was on the sidewalk. Since when can't I speak, he said. He took care not to let anyone in the cars cruising by see him move his lips. The wino's bottle crackled in its paper bag and swung up in an arc to his mouth. The wino looked at Sammy and put his index and middle fingers facing in against his lips momentarily. *Got a cigarette?* Sammy shook his head. Then, he raised his right hand above his head with the thumb pointing down and jerked it toward his open mouth. *Drink up.* The wino's face split in two in a wide grin. Sammy gave a thumbs up. *Carry on.*

It happened more slowly with women. He managed to say Yeah, No, and No shit? to a solidly-built middle-aged woman who took him into Vaughn. Her truck was clean and she handed him a couple of beers when he got out. But the next day, only a grunt came out when a younger woman driving a small red Japanese car picked him up. She was dark-haired and pretty, wearing pink-collar work clothes, maybe only five years older than Sammy. She stiffened, but Sammy pointed to his throat, waved his hand, shook his finger and then joined both of his hands in a namaste sign. *I can't speak. I'm not dangerous. I am very sorry.* She tightened her thin lips, gave an icy smile, and kept her eyes on the road. His tongue, legs and hands felt thick and clumsy, and he felt a drop of sweat fall from his right armpit onto his tee shirt.

One morning, he woke up in a box car. The floor was stamped iron crisscrossed with a pattern of waffle indentations in which a sticky petroleum-based substance pooled. He had taken six pallets from the edge of the freight yard and arranged them in a rectangle in one of the corners of the car to make a sleeping platform. He put his pack in the corner and lay down with his feet towards the end-wall. If you sleep with your head against the end wall, the old tramp in Washington had told him, it will crack open like an egg if they couple the car or run it over the hump. He had fallen asleep as soon as the sun went down and dreamt that the woman in the truck had picked him up again. He had said, I love you and then, I love you again. She had fed him a fish stew, geoduck clams, crabs, tomatoes, halibut, cod, onions, and garlic in a fish stock with bread, and then he had fallen asleep next to her in the passenger's seat with his head on her shoulder as she drove. When he opened his eyes, sunlight was streaming through both of the boxcar doors. Out the door to his right, he could see tanker cars, hoppers, and a few container cars. Out the other he saw hills, scrub, a big earth, and a big sun. Almost directly below the floor of the boxcar, ten or twelve guys were burning pallet wood in a fifty-gallon barrel. When Sammy stuck his nose out, a skinny old white guy with sunken cheeks and stubble looked up from the group and beckoned, *Out of bed,* but he was smiling. Sammy jumped onto the gravel. As he walked toward the group, another guy put his index and middle fingers – parallel and palm face in – to his lips as the wino had done. Sammy shook his head. A stocky, dark-skinned guy with a flat nose and long black hair did the same with his thumb and forefinger. *Mota?* Sammy shook his head again. The group laughed silently.

The old guy waved one hand in a semicircle around him with his elbow straight and the palm face down, then used his left hand to chop the semicircle in quarters. A plump, red-faced guy missing the middle and ring fingers on his right hand beckoned, and the dark-haired guy held up a cup of coffee, offering it to Sammy. Two guys made room for him. Sammy picked up a cinderblock, moved it to the now-empty space in the circle, and sat down.

That day, they taught him the sign for *coming* (hand out straight, palm up, beckon and throw air over your shoulder), *going* (start with upper arm parallel to ground, lower arm at ninety degrees pointed up, palm vertical, slice down and flick wrist), *I, you* and *he* (point with one finger), *we, you-all, they* (point with two), *together* (index fingers of both hands next to each other, stomach height, parallel to floor; move back and forth rapidly), *asshole* (form circle with thumb and forefinger, move hand away from body toward pinkie to form an air tube) and *bullshit* (forearms in front of body one on top of other parallel with ground, hands opposite each other. Make bull horns with one hand, open and shut other hand rapidly). When the sun reached a quarter of the way to mid-sky, one guy put his hands on his knees, stood up, banged an imaginary hammer against an air plank, and walked away. Another washed an imaginary dish. A third took a swig from an imaginary bottle, and everyone laughed. In fifteen minutes it was just Sammy and the fire. Sammy stashed his pack in a ditch at the edge of the yards, found a garbage bag, and began looking for bottles. It was sixty-five degrees and the sky was bluer than he had ever known it to be. He felt that he could glean bottles and cans forever.

The next morning, they taught him *what* (palms in front of chest, elbows bent), *where* (elbow bent, index finger vertical moving back and forth, searching), and the F-word (middle finger bent, penetrating a ring made by the thumb and forefinger of the other hand). Sammy had brought a can of coffee and some Wonder Bread from the Safeway; another guy had brought some government cheese. They sat on five-gallon drums, cinder blocks, and unburned pallets with their hands or elbows on their knees. To Sammy's left was a coupling between his boxcar and a hopper car. To the right was a row of tanker cars. Beyond that, the desert, the sky and town. The fire obviated the need to look at each other too often. Sammy noticed that the guy who had asked for *mota* and a younger white guy were gone, but two other guys had taken their place. The sky remained the same.

He stayed for two weeks. He learned *this* (index finger points at palm), *cojones* (hands at chest level hold two testicle-sized balls), *that* (sweep one palm with another, point with sweeping palm at ninety degrees outward), *cunnilingus* (lick space formed by v-shaped index and middle finger face in against mouth), *big* (hands apart, palms face-in), *long* (right index finger traces line from tip of left index finger across shoulders, then right arm extends ninety degrees), *small* (like *big*, only palms move together), *man* (right hand describes a baseball cap visor), *woman* (right hand thumbs-up sign moves from mouth to stomach height, describing a breast), *bone* (hands facing inward, index fingers and middle fingers forming two two-pronged claws), *blood* (hands at chest level, palms crossed; outer hand trickles down with fingers rippling), *see* (index finger and middle finger extended facing in; touch eye with middle finger), *hear* (same with hand facing out, middle finger touches ear). Guys came and went, but the old guy was always there. He seemed to take a liking to Sammy. He would make room next to himself for Sammy to sit. When the conversation got fast, he would repeat it, slowed down, for Sammy. He told him that, when he was Sammy's age, he had been in the army. His name was pronounced by extending the first and second finger of the speaker's right hand and shaking the wrist forty-five degrees up and down twice.

At the end of the morning of the fourteenth day, the old guy told the group that he would leave shortly. Sammy signed, *Where are you going?* The hands said, *I'll come back.*
When? Later. How much later? Stop! The lessons were over.

From there, Sammy took the BN south. A track walker told him *This one will take you to Belen. You can get another train south from there.* On the running board beside the coupling between two hopper cars, he found a pamphlet titled How To Lose Weight. Avoid pork and red meat. Exercise for at least thirty minutes each day. Stand up and stretch every forty-five minutes. Get no more than seven hours' sleep a night. He opened the pamphlet book-like, face down and sat on it. It did not provide much of a cushion, but it kept the wind from blowing up through the expanded metal grate. He sat with his back against the wall of the car, his knees bent and his heels resting on the bar before the coupling. A foot and a half to his right and to his left there was open space; in front of his feet, the metal ball and the metal socket joining the car he sat on with the adjacent car. The train was made up at three-thirty in the afternoon. He sat down on the book at four. The train didn't leave until nine. He shifted his weight every half-hour or so. He tried sitting cross-legged, lying on his back with his feet propped on the ladder that climbed up the side of the car, kneeling on his insteps, and lying in the fetal position. Each time he shifted, he was comfortable for a few minutes, but each position began to hurt after a while. After it left the yard, the train moved slowly. For a couple of hours in the early morning, it pulled onto a siding and sat for a couple of hours. Even though there was little wind, it was cold. There was no sound and no moon, the Milky Way formed a band across the sky, and the stars seemed so big that they overlapped. Sammy told himself, You will never come here again. The train reached Truth or Consequences around six. Paused at a crossing, he saw two brown-skinned kids carrying school bags. He tried to shout, Take me to your leader, Earthlings, but hissing noises came out instead. Then he waved and signed, *you guys come from far away?* The bigger of the kids laughed and pointed, and the smaller stood with locked knees staring at him with wide, brown eyes.

The train was taken apart at the terminal town. The river, which ran past the freight yard, was like a prison wall. The channel itself was poured cement. A barbed-wire fence ran parallel to the American bank as far as Sammy could see. After that, there was a strip of no-man's land accessible only by ICE vehicles, and then a wall made of steel slats topped with razor wire that pitched south. The wall was unbroken east to west except for a point a quarter mile to his right, where cars and trucks lined up to cross the bridge.

He had climbed down an embankment next to an on-ramp to take a piss when he first saw them. Six people crawling out of a culvert. Two men, a woman carrying a baby and two toddlers – dirty, dark, broad-featured. He waved and hissed, and they scuttled back into the culvert. He finished his piss and walked into town.

He went back to the culvert at the same time the next day. Another group crawled out. He held his hands up and beckoned. They stayed where they were, but they looked at him blankly without smiling or saying anything. He saw four younger men, an older woman, a young mother, and a few small kids. He signed, *Water. Over here.* He placed two plastic gallon jugs that he had filled at a hose bib in the freight yard on the ground, waved and walked away. He saw the older woman nod *thank you* right before he scrambled up the bank of the highway, out of sight of the culvert.

He remembered not to hiss. That scared people. Sometimes a few squeaks came out from the back of his throat when he signed.

He brought two more gallons of water to the culvert that night.

On the same trip, he took the empty jugs, filled them and returned them to the same place. The next day, he found a five-gallon jug in a dumpster behind the Home Depot. The day after that, he found that Food City threw old bread into *their* dumpster. A few fast-food joints threw out old hamburgers and fries that they could not sell. He developed a rhythm. He slept in the yards, stashed his pack and picked up cans during the day. Just before the sun went down, he would leave as much water and food that he could carry at the culvert. He would come back in the morning, before he started the day's work of gleaning. There was rarely anyone there at night, but the food was gone in the mornings, and the water containers were empty. Sometimes, he found things that people had left behind when he visited at night – candy wrappers, a sock, a tee shirt, condoms, scrunchies, pink or blue pacifiers. He stacked the things that he thought might be useful just inside the culvert and took the rest away.

He would sign to people he met at the culvert, *Where are you going? Where are you coming from? How long have you been travel-ing?* The answers were easy to understand. *Ecuador. California. Tres meses*, three fingers. When he saw someone more than once, he would sign, *Why are you still here?* The answer to that was always, *Esperando.*

It took him three days to work up the courage to ask one young mother what her name was. He would never have asked her out loud, but it was easier to sign than to speak. He pointed to himself, wrote, "Sammy" on a notebook page, then pointed to her and held up his palms. *Rosa. Why are you still here?*, he signed. *Esperanda.* The top of her head was no higher than his shoulder. She had black hair, black eyes and a flat, slightly hooked nose. Her teeth were bright white and she smiled when she answered. She could not have been older than him. She held an infant in her arms and a toddler boy hugged her leg. Sammy signed, *How old is this one? Nueve meses.*

Sammy pointed to the toddler and flexed his biceps. *That one is macho. No, peceño. What is this one named? Lupe. Can I hold her? Seguro.* Their forearms slid against each other when she handed him the baby, and his stomach brushed against her breast. She smelled like lemon, people, and something he didn't know. Women?, he thought. Mexico? He put one hand underneath the baby's head, and another beneath her butt. The baby's eyes remained closed, but her breath made her neck rise and fall, barely perceptibly. Snot had congealed at the entrance to her nostrils, which gave her breath a soft grinding sound. She was wrapped in a dirty towel with one arm swaddled and the other exposed and lying on top of her body with the fingers extended. The toddler began to tug at his mother's leg. Sammy handed the baby back. He signed, *Beautiful. Gracias.*

When he kissed his bicep that night, he saw Rosa's teeth, eyes, and nose. He imagined buying an almond orchard, building a house for her, and making a tire swing for the kids. He imagined lying next to her at night when the kids were asleep, learning enough Spanish to say I love you, possibly making a child of their own. The kid would not have a father who strangled him, and would not be sent to a school where they tie you down for chewing gum, and the other kids pin you to your bed and jerk off on you. He would eat almonds, swing on the tire swing with his brother and his sister, and babble as much as he wanted in English and Spanish.

Perfume

Amy K. Genova

Her nostrils fill with soft-swollen scent: black cottonwoods, soil, the musky odor of her old dog in his slouching fur. Her fingertips, fragrant from pulling stray grass-shoots in her gravel driveway. The idling smoke in this poor side of town eddying the air with burning trash. Its smell pokes her chest, recalls the backyard red-bricked furnace of her childhood. Whirling on South Jersey street, perfumed by its crown of lilac bushes. Her yellow dress, a slack coat wrapped around her. Socks fallen with loose elastics. Wanting one of the well-kept tulip-shuttered houses to be a mother. Invite her home. A mother who would brush the tangle of her hair. Place a perfumed hand like a warm Valentine on her back. But Mother would be jealous, with a shriek that scolded out windows. When she slapped the girl, it took a while for her nose to stop bleeding. The headache to stop blooming. Mother shamed her for that delicate nose. But applied a bunched washcloth above her lip, *where the angels kiss*. All her life, the grown girl sought the scent of Mother. Around the long blocks collapsing with moss-roofed houses, pinched by abandoned

churches, through the flank of alley-ways with their odor of mildewed mattress, and blue morning glories clinging to chain-link
fences. only the fragrance of onion-oily dinner invites her to homes
she cannot go.

The hems of my long skirt

Amy K. Genova

I rave to the stars
Imagine protection for granddaughters
with a frenzy of arms
In bracelets of gold, stippled with delirium pink

I would be rich and consumed
Purchase paisley-dress holiness
and be adorned and adored
in Tree-of-life gold

I would my granddaughters be dervishes

Whirling skirts to unstitch gemstones
for men sow wealth from the pockets of children
buy islands and steal the silver-topped palaces of gypsies

Granddaughters, seed your own children.

John 8:32

Erin Ruble

The screen flickers behind her granddaughter's shoulder. Tiger Woods, closing another perfect swing. Joan's never golfed herself, but she likes a game with rules, where the penalties for violations are evenly applied. It's refreshingly unlike life.

Not that she's made a study of life. In fact, she finds it's best not to look too closely at it, though it is hard sometimes not to wonder at how she ended up here, in this place at the edge of the world. She used to like staying put, once.

A woman in an unflattering floral blouse and mauve slacks comes in and takes Joan's wrist, staring at her own watch. Apparently satisfied, she hands her a paper cup, then walks to the sink to fill a plastic pitcher. Joan peers into the tiny thing in her hand. Two capsules the size of horse pills clog the bottom. She fishes one out with slow fingers as the woman returns with a glass of water. The pills scrape against her throat as she swallows.

"Hand me my handbag, would you?" she asks her granddaughter when the woman leaves. She's not sure when the girl arrived. Lucy chatters away as Joan rummages through the compartments, but finally pauses and asks what she is looking for.

"My cigarettes. I put them in here last night."

"You quit smoking," Lucy says, which is absurd, but the cigarettes are definitely not in the bag. The maid must've taken them. This is the worst hotel she's ever stayed in.

Jim liked to rate hotels, had a whole list in his head, best to worst. He'd been through his share. He always had some new business, some grand scheme that he had to hustle for. Like the mushrooms he grew one summer in caves by the river. He might have made something off them, if the river hadn't flooded. Sometimes he talked as if the world itself was set against him. As if the harder he tried, the worse it all went.

How she loved that river though, a band of brown water a mile thick and as slow as a summer afternoon that's going to breed storms. Her sister Nadine used to dare her to swim across it. She never did—there were currents there that could foul a boat, let alone a girl, and who could swim a mile, anyway? But maybe that's why Jim got to her so easy, promising to take her across. He did too, all the way to Denver, where there's no river worth the name.

She can see him there now in his sharp suit, with his slicked-back hair and his smile—his smile's what did it, that and something in his eyes. Leaning back like he didn't have a care in the world, but watching everything, intent as a lean dog by the dinner table. He cared, all right.

Nadine never understood the draw, but then Nadine never liked edges. Joan asked her once what she thought Jesus was there to redeem if the world was so blasted good all the time. She said, "I know there's evil out there, Joan, I just don't choose to dwell on it." That was about the most penetrating thing she'd ever said, as far as Joan knew. She loved her sister, but the woman was flighty as a butterfly. She guessed that's how she could keep her disposition so cheerful. The only way to keep seeing goodness in this world may be to flit from one bright color to another, never staying long enough to see the wilt.

Of course Joan was one to talk about flitting, having trailed for years from state to state behind her husband and later, her son. Each new place Joan moved, she didn't know a soul, but that had been the point, hadn't it, maybe half or more of why she left with Jim in the first place. She couldn't stand all that knowingness at home. In Colorado, Oregon, Montana, when people asked her about the family she grew up in, she could just say, "I have one sister," and leave it at that. And that's all they'd ever know. It wasn't even lying.

Lucy pulls out her book bag, which is covered with pins that say things like "Whirled peas" and "Subvert the dominant paradigm.". Joan points to one that says only "John 8:32". Before she can ask, Lucy flashes that smile of hers and says, "It's from the Bible." Her intonation suggests she might as easily have said, "It's from the Hindu scriptures," or "It's ancient cuneiform from Mesopotamia." Joan's quite sure that Lucy's never been to Mass.

"It's a quote," Lucy says. She closes her eyes to help her get it right. "Then you will know the truth, and the truth will set you free." Her eyes open. "Isn't that beautiful?"

"Yes," Joan says, because she wants to see that smile again. Sure enough, it reappears. Lucy dives into her bag and takes out a paperback. She's wearing about fifteen plastic bracelets on each wrist, all different colors, and they click as she moves. "We're reading *To Kill a Mockingbird* in English. I have to write a report on it, and I know you grew up in Illinois, not Alabama, but it's kind of in the same time period, and I thought maybe I could interview you about it." She looks hopeful.

"There's nothing much to tell."

"But did you spit before a handshake like that? Or have secret knotholes? Or run around all afternoon with nobody watching you?"

No spit, but the kids would roam through the streets of Quincy, playing until the summer days faded to gilded evenings. They would feast on potatoes they'd cooked themselves over little fires in the park, and when it grew dark they would wash up on her front steps, where she would tell ghost stories until her father emerged. His hand would drop to her shoulder, his heavy fingers stained black from the type he set all day. Her mother, always flustered, hair escaping from her bun, would bustle over to kiss her goodnight.

Lucy listens but is back on the book again. "There's this guy named Boo Radley," she says, and Joan remembers. A crazy man running around peering into people's windows, and the talk. Of course people talk. That's all people do, is talk, and something like that—well.

She wants to tell Lucy that Harper Lee didn't know anything at all, making you think that the man wasn't crazy. Just misunderstood. Shy, maybe. Never mind that he stuck scissors into his father's leg, sent him to the hospital. Just a victim of small-minded prejudice.

Tripe, all of it. No one ever writes the truth, because no one wants the truth. She doesn't. She has been glad to let it run right through her fingers. She slipped up once, mentioning Eddy in front of her own boys, but otherwise, they never even knew they had an uncle. And why should they? All that stuff just weighs you down.

Nadine's got all those old photos from home. The two girls together, smiling in their bows and belled skirts, and Eddy in knickers and socks, always standing apart, always frowning, even then. He was four years older. He should've looked out for her, warned away guys like Jim. Though who would she have married then? She can't imagine living in Nadine's kind of sunshine.

She remembers once going out to the yard. He'd been there all day, and his knees were stained and damp. She sat down next to him on the leaves and followed his gaze to where a squirrel perched near the base of a tree. "He's got a nut there," Eddy said, his voice a little hoarse. He tilted his chin slightly toward a trunk where another squirrel clung, watching the first. "He keeps digging it up when that one gets too close, and burying it again."

Joan watched the squirrel tense, shift, freeze. "It seems like a lot of work."

Eddy nodded, very slightly. "He should forget," he said softly. "You don't have to worry about it anymore if you've forgotten."

He told Joan things. Secrets, like the squirrel. Even when the others couldn't get near him, she always could. Until she couldn't.

Lucy asks what she's looking for as she picks up her bag. "My cigarettes," she tells her. "You can't smoke anymore," Lucy says, as if she's said this before. As if quitting were an option. Joan can picture the cellophane sliding smooth under her fingers, the smell of the tobacco when she opens the box. The first pull, how it fills her lungs and her body comes a little alive again. Petty of the girl to deny her such a small thing. Yes, she knows it's bad for her, but in her experience, even the things they tell you are good—marriage, children, new starts—aren't all they're cracked up to be. You think with enough love you'll make the world safe but sooner or later it isn't enough and the love you used to get back just runs out.

She can see Jim there at his desk, knocking back drinks after dinner with his parents. He'd stood before the pictures in their front room, studying the faces of his brothers: the admiral; the diplomat; and the war hero, who drowned on a submarine in the Pacific while Jim's bad heart kept him in Seattle. Jim had never even made it through college. She'd slipped her arm into his but he'd turned to her with flat eyes and she'd stepped back, her throat suddenly dry.

He talked too loud at dinner, took up too much space, and when they got home, the look in his eyes—she ran to the kitchen and stood there just trying to breathe.

That was the beginning.

Then his emphysema set in, just when his wholesale business at last began to take off. The bills piled up and the orders went unfilled and he couldn't even get out the door without coughing. He'd sit with the bottle and lay into whoever was nearby.

Of the three boys, Luke usually got it the most. Mark fought back, wild from the start. Sailed through school on a lick and a prayer. She loved him hard, so hard that something in her broke when he told her he was going away, like she was one more obstacle to climb over on his way to freedom. She stopped trying then, stopped even trying to shield the two sons left at home. Instead she started listening to news on the radio. There was always some disaster somewhere: a war, a purge, a flood.

When the Mississippi flooded, now that was something to behold. All that brown water. You never knew how fast it could be, or how strong. It's the slow things that get you, every time. Water rising an inch here or there, a man starting to frown, age slipping up on you in little bursts as the years roll over. They add up, until suddenly you're standing on your roof with a suitcase in your hand looking at a world you don't know.

Luke left too, after a few years. It took a while for her to notice that Matt had stayed. Still young when Jim turned mean, he'd learned to fade into the background: do well in school, do his chores, give no one cause to notice him. But he'd sit in the kitchen while she made dinner, working on his own projects. He came home on school vacations. When Jim died, Matt invited her to move near them, and then he had Lucy.

A woman comes in, smiling too brightly, saying "we" when she means "you." She fusses around Joan for a minute, then leaves, taking the tray of food that smells like plastic. This whole place is like that, chemical scents and beige wallpaper and contrived pictures of children in cheap frames. Even the grass on the TV looks too green. It's all ersatz, like wartime margarine. Like a family with two daughters, and no son.

It got to where she didn't even want to visit her parents in Quincy. Nadine didn't mind it, all the neighbors knowing, but Nadine was young enough not to remember the worst of it. She didn't even much remember the night everyone in the house woke up to hear Molly Burke, who lived next door, screaming. They rushed out to find Eddy cowering in a corner of the back yard and Molly's father advancing on him with a crowbar. Joan could just make out from the shouting that Eddy had been peering at her friend through the window as she slept, may even have pushed the window open. Molly's father wanted blood; Molly would not look at Joan or any of them.

Joan had somehow managed to wave them all back and had approached Eddy, slowly, as if he were one of his own wild creatures. "Eddy?" she'd said, her heart jumping in her chest. Molly was wailing now and Eddy had tear tracks stitching his crumpled face. He was fifteen, all legs and arms and ears, the pieces of a man assembled but none fitting quite right. Joan inched closer. She knew he didn't like to be touched, knew it, but she could hear her heart over the voices of all the neighbors and he looked more frightened than she.

All it took was a hand on his arm, just a touch, and he recoiled, the confusion on his face turning to actual hate. "You're one of them now," he said, and ran off. She never learned who "they" were. And Molly never spoke to her again.

Nadine tried to get Joan to visit Eddy in Springfield. She said they were giving him electric shocks, but the treatment didn't help much. He drew pictures in his spare time. It makes Joan mad, the waste of it. A grown man drawing with crayons like a child.

He's dead now, these thirty years and more. Joan's parents are dead, too, and half her friends. You get to a time in your life where that's the way of things. You're supposed to accept it. Our Father who art in heaven. Forgive us our trespasses. She always loved the rhythm of the old prayers. She used to think they were incantations, wards against misfortune. Now she wonders. You can ask for for-giveness, but God rewards the good and punishes wrongdoers, that's what they were taught. *Though I walk through the valley of the shadow of death.* She lives in that valley now, breathes its twilight air.

Where are her cigarettes?

The TV flickers as Tiger Woods swings. She had not realized golf was on. Lucy, her back to the game, is telling a story about school. Joan can't quite follow the thread of it. The words loop like birds catching thermals, way up at the edge of your sight. The meaning glints and then disappears again.

Amazing how much that girl can talk, even through the braces that glint on her teeth. Joan imagines her backward, the curly red-dish hair drawing into pigtails, then a bob, the braces disappearing and the teeth too, until she's a baby rocking in a green plastic swing in the tiny house Joan rented in Portland.

There were other houses, with Jim and after him, changing over and over as their fortunes ebbed and swelled and ebbed again. New rooms always felt smaller before the furniture came in. You could see all the scuff marks, dents, chipped window sills, rust stains on porcelain. At one time that might have comforted her, signs of all those lives carried out in the same spaces, but now the memory just tires her out, like this desert of a prairie, all thorns and sage. No rivers worth the name. The Mississippi, now that's water. All that brown motion, the hidden currents, the eddies swirling and swirling, going nowhere.

Forgive us our trespasses as we forgive those who trespass against us. But what if He didn't forgive? What if the mist that clouded Eddy's brain was a sign of His judgment? Or that night in Molly's yard a test that Joan failed? *For the word of God is quick, and powerful, and sharper than any two-edged sword.* But what could be sharper than a double-edged sword? Eddy changing from the brother she had loved, the town full of whispers, Jim arriving with his white-walled tires and the breath of other places, Jim's glares, Luke drawing inward, Matt going invisible and Mark wild, all of them now with babies who scream as they're pushed into the world, the whole spiral of it, living and dying and living again, all springing from a single shoot.

She's carried the squirrel's secret with her for 80 years. When she dies, it'll be gone. Except maybe there's an oak tree growing where he buried that nut. She never thought to look.

Someone left a paper cup on the nightstand; she knocks it over as she fumbles for some water. What lousy kind of motel would leave tiny cups like this around? Jim would have laid into this one. He saw the worst of the country, traveling like he did. He kept himself sharp, though, hair slicked back, smile like he knew what was coming for him and was just daring it to arrive. Maybe they were both that way. Maybe that's how everything starts.

Her eyes fall on the TV, and she lifts the remote to turn up the volume. Golf, but the tournament is ending. It's too bad she missed it. If only she had realized it was on.

Toast

Olga J. Hebert

I beeline through the kitchen
in rumpled pajamas and worn slippers,
ignore the smell of bacon and toast
as I pour cream, then coffee into the rounded bowl
of my Polish pottery mug, blue patterned,
pretty but sturdy, hefty in my hand.

I click off television news blaring in the corner
to hear him singing in the shower,
turn away from the table
with its plate of crumbs congealed in runny egg yolk,
stare out at a thin ray of pink forming
on the horizon – a red line.

Smoke rises from the toaster. I burn my fingers
pulling out a slice of charred bread
that bears the image of my mother at the sink

scraping the black off burned toast –
good enough for her to eat –
bitterness spread with butter.

Dear Mother Bear

Janet McKeehan-Medina

teach me the ways of hibernation.
How to fold in upon myself during glaciated winters,
be the source of light and heat that sparks vitality.
Red embers that crackle,
beneath a pellucid frozen dreamscape,
nourished by the roots of creation.

To be quiet and calm as the world whizzes by,
and eternity lives in a breath.
Comforted by the earth that shelters me,
thoughtful in stagnation, suspended animation,
yet aware of the stars, the moon, the vastness,
the love that fills the spaces in-between.

Let me remain steady stable serene
like icicles that hang on a branch,
Melting slowly into other forms of being.

Molded in the rays of resurrecting sun,
my outer shell thaws,
revealing what I am.

A bad day,
production-wise, in the
sugarhouse

Andrew Carlo

We built this sugarhouse in the woods, but just at the edge of the woods so someone could stand here and look out this window and watch this field.

We built it in the woods for the obvious reason: that's where the maple trees are. But we built it at the edge of the woods, and also at the edge of the field that's next to the woods because the field is where the light is. And across the field and down the hill – that's where home is. So, when you look out the window of the sugarhouse, you see the hill and the field – and if the day is clear you see home –but mostly what you see is the light.

We built it many years ago, and back then we were young and ignorant of most things (at least I was), but even in our ignorance we had enough sense to know that it's good to watch a field, and to watch the light on a field, and to see home way off in the distance, and to think about the things that come to mind from the window of a sugarhouse. We planned it that way and then we built it that way.

But, this brief summary of building the sugarhouse might imply a good deal of foresight and planning; a careful consideration of the aesthetics of the place, and that's not exactly right. The truth is, there was just a little foresight, but not much, and we considered aesthetics hardly at all, and there was a plan, but only a minimally-sufficient plan to build a sugarhouse.

But, on an April day many years later, the plan seems to be working fairly well.

Today the light is bright and the air is still. The snow, gone from the field, but the field itself still frozen and hard. The air above the field is filled with light and home is way off across the field. It's good to watch the field today. It's pretty much exactly the way we planned it.

Of course the main reason we built the sugarhouse was so someone could make maple syrup. Today, if I do what I'm supposed to (which is mainly to keep the fire going in the arch, keep the sap boiling in the pans, and don't burn the pans) that someone will be me. By all indications, I'm on-track to make some syrup today.

But out the window the light is bright today. And across the field I see home. And on the hill the stubble of last year's mowing lies flat and smooth against the ground. It glistens in the light. And the air is perfectly still but it shimmers in the light. And something approaches, coming through the shimmer.

It's the dog, coming through the shimmer.

She approaches with her nose in the stubble. She searches. She finds. She inspects the thing. She smells it. She paws it with her paw. She drops to the ground and rolls in it. She grinds the thing into the fur on the side of her neck.

Best guess is it's something half-frozen, and aromatic, and dead. Best guess is she'll wear the aroma for the rest of the day. Best guess is I'll remember this moment, this shimmering air, this glistening stubble when I scratch behind her ear this evening, and smell the thing from the field.

And then a child approaches, coming through the shimmer.

He wears red soccer shoes, camo long johns, earbuds. He rolls a piece of culvert into position at the top of the hill. With the snow gone and the ground frozen and the grass flattened, the rolling conditions are pretty good today.

There's something about the light on a day like this.

I watch the field veiled in the over-bright sunlight, and it's this light – I think – that tempts my mind to shift. My mind shifts and goes to another time, to another field, and to a child of that other field. My mind shifts to a child who also pushed a culvert to the top of a hill.

For a moment I touch that old steel culvert, I feel the slope of the hill beneath my old sneakers, I see the shimmer of the sunlight.

And time is stuck there for a moment.

And when it unsticks, an extraordinary transformation occurs. That old steel culvert disappears; that old Connecticut hill disappears; that child disappears, and in his place there stands.....me, a middle-aged man in a sugarhouse, standing beside a window, watching a child push a culvert and a dog roll in something dead.

And then the field is filled with light again.

And my mind shifts to a time before memory, to children who lived and died before memory, to children who are gone now and will be gone forever. It shifts to fields of ancient times: fields that I never knew; fields that grew up to forests; fields that were buried under highways. Children and fields who had their time, who lived and died, and now their time is done.

And then my mind shifts back again, to this field and this time, and to this child, pushing.

It's time now in the field. It's the child's time. The culvert is in position. The child drops to his knees. He crouches, he squirms in. His feet stick out one end and his hands stick out the other.

This is not something I would advise anyone to do.

But what right do I have to object? What right do I have to walk out there and suggest to a child that he weigh the potential benefits of culvert-rolling, if any, against the potential risks? That would not go over well.

Does it matter that the child who became me once rolled in a culvert?

No.

All that matters now is the child. I matter not at all. I'm an irrelevant middle-aged man. I've forgotten everything I ever knew about culvert-rolling. I have no standing in this field. I have no grounds to object. (And after a painful learning curve, I know this child well enough. He's stubborn as hell. I couldn't stop him if I tried.)

I can tell by the motion of the hands and the feet that he's settling himself in – inside the culvert. He's all business in there. And then I can tell by a little shudder of the culvert that he leans his body forward into the downhill wall and the culvert starts to roll. It rolls over the crest of the hill. The dog follows, barking.

Now there's not much more to see. The culvert is gone, what's left is the frozen field and the shimmer of light.

Now there is this field, this light, but once there was my own field, my own hill, my own culvert. And just like today, someone watched through a window while a child did something stupid out in a field.

Maybe there was a shimmer then too. Maybe that person who watched me through the window, maybe she thought of another time when everything shimmered in the sunlight for her. If she did, that was her time, then I had my time in the culvert, and now this time belongs to the child who just rolled over the crest of the hill.

There should be a connection here: this child and me and that other person at the window.

Are we all not parts of a whole?

You'd think so, but what should be a whole is not a whole. What should be a whole is so torn, and frayed, and tangled, and so full of holes itself that to call it a whole is a real stretch.

If that person who watched me through the window, my mother, if she were here right now she might complete the connection. And if my father who was also there at the window, but who did not watch, if he were here right now, he might complete the connection too. But they are both long-gone now. They are many decades long-gone. So the questions for me are: What remains of this so-called connection? What remains for my children to know the connection and to make something of it? And what remains of the connection for me?

I have no idea. All I know is that the connection is not connected. In fact, I don't see any connection at all. All I see is the old-mown stubble of last-year's grass. All I see is the shimmer in the April sunlight. All I hear is the dog barking frantically at something down below.

This hill gets pretty steep about half-way down. It starts gradually where the culvert disappears over the top, and then it steepens, and then it runs out at the bottom into a little wet swale that's probably a sheet of ice right now. It's a lot steeper and a lot longer than my own hill back when I was young. A culvert could pick up a lot of speed on the steep part, and then there's nothing to stop it when it hits the sheet of ice. Then it would just continue rolling towards the treeline. That could be trouble for whoever's inside. Just another trouble in a long line of troubles.

I think about my parents at their window, watching and not watching. I wonder about them and about their troubles. Was there trouble for them in their home? Was there trouble for them in the time of their memories? Was there trouble in their time before memory? If there was, the remains of it are pretty faint now (just like the remains of everything else). But maybe that's the way trouble should be. Maybe that's how we move on.

Finally, at the bottom of the hill, I see motion. The child is up. He's walking. Not very effectively, but at least he's up. But he's still in the culvert.

Now there's a vertical black-plastic cylinder. With legs. A plastic cylinder, walking a crooked walk, walking the way people walk when they're inside a culvert, or when they've been rattled by rolling, or when they've just injured their head (which is often referred to as a noggin in such cases).

But the culvert walks.

And maybe it's the light, but it looks like the culvert walks not on the stubble, but somewhere above the stubble. It looks like the culvert walks just above the almost-white ground, in the almost-golden air. It walks where the two meet in the shimmer. And something is there.

I must have missed it before but I see it now.

I see a thread floating there like a strand of cobweb.

The thread runs from the child in the culvert. It runs to me in the field of my memory. It runs to me now in my middle-age looking out this window. It runs to those people, my parents, standing beside their window. It runs to the ancient time in the haze before memory. And then it runs back to this child, my son.

What is that thread?

I think it's just this:

We, who watch over the child as he rolls out of sight, we love the child.

And this too:

And we, the children doing something stupid out in a field, we are loved, even as we tumble towards the treeline.

That's it. That's all.

It's not much, but it's a start. It's a connection.

I wonder what my parents would say. They always had something to say. They were talkers, and writers, and readers, and thinkers. They believed in connections. They studied connections, taught them, and wove them together. They carried the past with them and offered it to the future. They tied themselves to each, the past and the future, with a million fragile threads, a million little connections. And from all those threads they wove a thing that you might call a whole (although the remains of it are pretty frayed now). So I enlist them now in this one simple connection. I enlist them now without knowing what they might have said (but knowing that they won't say anything anymore unless they say it here, through me. Which I guess is also part of the connection.)

They were so different from us, being of their ancient time.

But they did what they could, just like us. They struggled, they stumbled, but they didn't fall, just like us. We don't fall either. No one does.

They might have had a thing or two to say about that. They might have had a thing or two to say to my children but they never got the chance.

What would they have said?

I watch the field. I watch the thread. I watch the culvert with legs. I see it stumble but it doesn't fall. I see the question. It hangs there over the field without an answer.

At times like this it occurs to me that I might write a little family history project.

(After I finish this syrup.)

Randy Larose's Life of Crime

Masha Harris

The keys jangled loud enough to wake the dead: a big carabiner full of them dangling from the ignition of the livestock truck. They jangled because Randy's goddam leg wouldn't stop shaking. He steadied it now, and the night grew quiet. But the quiet made him nervous, and his leg set to shaking again, and the keys set to jangling.

Randy Larose was, according to his mémé, "a squirrelly little fucker." She'd called him that from the time he could walk, all the way up to the day she died. She was fond of him, though, unlike his mother, who called him "that boy," or his father – who best he could tell hadn't called him anything at all since about 1988. His teachers called him "a problem child;" his pediatrician prescribed Ritalin, which he took up till he aged out of his mom's health insurance, at which point he was on his own again. His friends called him Randy, and his girlfriend – well, she stopped calling him altogether.

He kicked at the floor around the pedals. Shouldn't have been thinking about Jessica; that always got him down. This wasn't their first time on the outs. He shouldn't worry about it – she'd be back.

Randy clicked the key forward a notch, and the clock glowed orange on the dash of the old vehicle. It was 2:37. He wasn't sleepy – Randy didn't sleep much – but he wished they'd hurry up anyway. He could be home playing Call of Duty. He could make some mozzarella sticks. He knew you were supposed to make them in the oven, but what the hell did those people have against the microwave, anyway? They tasted just fine that way.

He opened the door and jumped down, walking around the truck, kicking at the tires. He started to open the door to the back, but it made too much noise. Rene had told him to stay quiet, stay under the radar. He was trying his best, but it wasn't easy.

Alls you gutta do is drive the truck to Rouses Point. I'll meet you there an' drive you back.

"Alls I gutta do is wait three hours for them to show," Randy grumbled, seriously exaggerating how long he'd been there. Rene had told him two o'clock at the earliest, probably later, and Randy had rolled in about 2:10. But it *felt* like he'd been there three hours.

He walked down the dirt road a little ways, but then started to wonder if that wouldn't be considered staying under the radar. Fists clenched tight, he headed back to the truck, opened the door, and climbed in. Clicked the key forward again: 2:52.

He didn't have a fancy device to keep his mind off things, just an old flip phone. You could call or text and that was it, which didn't do him much good in the middle of the night. He pulled up his last conversation with Jessica – another mistake.

I just feel like we're going nowhere
and
Maybe we'd both be better off with somebody else
He slammed the phone shut. "Fuckin' a."

Randy glared into the rear view mirror, waiting for headlights, and it took him a while to register the truck coming towards him not from behind, not from the main road, but rather from ahead of him. It was another livestock truck, newer and larger than the one Randy had borrowed from the farm. (Randy wondered if "borrowed" was technically the right word.) The truck cut its headlights and pulled up behind him, so close they nearly hit.

He climbed out of the truck and was disappointed to find the man climbing out of the other one was not Rene. Instead, it was a tall, muscular blond guy a solid decade younger than himself. He reminded Randy of some kind of Greek god, shining and golden.

"Sup?" He nodded, just as Randy blurted, "Where's Rene?"

The Greek god blinked at him. "The fuck kind of name is Rainy?"

Randy blinked back. He didn't see any problem. He knew about a half a dozen Renes. Then he shrugged. "I'm Randy."

"At least not everybody in this shitbag state's named after the weather."

From this Randy concluded that the Greek god was not going to tell him his name, and also that he was not very nice.

The Greek god began to set up the plywood floor to get the cattle from one truck to the other. Not to be outdone, Randy started setting up the blinders on either side to finish the chute. He might not have huge muscles and a statuesque physique, but he was strong and wiry and proudly got done first – though he couldn't help but notice the Greek god's work went a lot smoother and a lot quieter.

When he was done, he watched the guy finish up, then peered into his truck. Half a dozen Holstein calves blinked back at him. "Hey, you gut calves in here!"

The Greek god grunted and encouraged the calves to make their way out of his truck and into Randy's.

"They'll be needin' their mamas though," Randy mused. "They comin' in a diffren' truck?" Without even realizing it, he herded the calves up into his truck, with a grace that could have landed him a job dancing in a big city like Burlington. The Greek god hadn't answered. "Hey, I assed you a question. The other cows comin' on a diffren' truck? Rene only told me 'bout the one truck."

The Greek god turned to face him, with a look of malice that suddenly softened. "Don't worry about the calves," he reassured him. "We have people taking care of that."

Randy felt better as he made sure the calves were snug. The Greek god helped him get the portable chute stowed. "Now listen. Don't speed – but don't go too slow, either, it looks suspicious. Five above is just about right."

Randy nodded.

"If anyone stops you, tell them whose farm you work at, tell them it's their truck, make like they asked you to make this trip. If they ask too many questions, play dumb."

Randy nodded again.

"Shouldn't be hard," the Greek god muttered. "Okay, you know where you're going?"

"Pillsbury Road, Rouses Point," Randy recited. "There's a pull-off on the left."

"Good. Good luck."

"Have a good 'un," Randy said. He climbed back into the truck, started it up, and headed back to Route 105.

Randy didn't get much call to leave Franklin County, and even less call to leave the state, but tonight he would do both. He tried to hold his breath on the bridge that took him to Alburgh, one county over, but his lungs weren't very good, and he couldn't do it the whole way. He hated bridges, and hated them even more when he couldn't hold his breath across them. He pounded the steering wheel with an open palm, trying to get the discomfort out.

Alburgh was a *peninsula* – he remembered this word from school because it sounded like "penis" and that's what peninsulas looked like, too, attached but dangling. Anyway, point was, because Alburgh was a penis-ula, he had to cross two bridges, which sucked ass. The bridge to New York was even bigger than the one to Alburgh, and as he drove around the bends, through the little town, past the old brick school whose sign read *Alburg lementary School*, and back out onto the farmlands, all he could think was how much he didn't want to cross that bridge.

And then, there he was. He took as deep a breath as he could. He ran out of breath at the halfway point, right where he crossed the state line. Inhaled again, held it, and made it across.

Randy didn't know Rouses Point at all, but he was a good driver and, like any good driver, had a pretty good handle on following directions. He found Pillsbury Road easy enough, and soon came to the pull-off. Rene's pickup was already there waiting for him. He turned off the livestock truck but left the keys in it, as instructed. He hopped out and climbed into the passenger seat of Rene's truck.

"Hey man, sup?"

Rene nodded at him. "Everything go okay?"

"Yeah. That guy was kind of a dick, man, I thought you were goin' ta be there!"

"Naw, they gut different guys doin' different things. I'm just suppose ta drive you back."

"Yeah I mean he wasn' that bad, just not very friendly."

Rene grunted.

"What's goin' ta happen to the calves now? That guy said people were goin' ta take care of 'em?"

"Eeyut. Somebody'll be by for the truck soon. We don't gutta wait."

"Okay," Randy said, but he wasn't sure he was happy about it. He didn't like the idea of leaving the calves there alone. What if they got stolen?

But Rene had already put the truck in gear, and was on his way back to the main road. They came to an intersection, with a sign that simply read *Canada, straight ahead; Vermont, right.*

"Shit," Rene said, and ducked his head a bit. In a pull-off in front of the sign sat a Statie.

Randy had always thought cop cars looked a little bit like bugs, big beetles or something, or else like snakes, lying in wait and prepared to strike. On instinct he also said "Shit" and ducked. He watched Rene watch the rear view, but they made their turn and approached the bridge without the cop stopping them. Randy took a deep breath – though he didn't mind bridges as much when he wasn't the one driving – and soon they were back in Vermont, out of the Statie's reach.

The rest of the drive was uneventful. Randy managed to hold his breath almost the whole way over the other, smaller bridge. He was thrilled to see Rene and jabbered at him the whole way back, talking about work, the farm, and Call of Duty, which Rene, like nearly everyone else, had stopped playing several years ago. When they got closer to the farm, however, Randy became mournful.

"Jessica, man, I don' know what I'm goin' ta do. I love her so much but she says we ain't going nowhere."

"Well if you ain't, you ain't."

"But I gutta try, man. That's what I'm sayin'. I don' wan' ta let her go."

"I'unno, man."

"And she don' know how good things are goin' ta be. I gut dreams, man. I'm goin' ta be somebody."

"I hear ya, Randy, but it ain't up to you. It's up to her."

Randy sighed, wishing his best friend wasn't so wise. "You're right."

When they got back to the farm, Rene pulled a roll of bills from his back pocket and asked, "Wha' did they tell you your cut was for tonight?"

"Sevenny-five."

Rene handed him four twenties and a ten. "Here's ninety."

"Wow! Thanks!"

Rene put the rest of the bills back in his pocket, looking uncomfortable.

"What's wrong?" Randy asked.

Rene sat for a long moment, and Randy could tell he was thinking hard. "I don' think you should do somethin' like this again," he finally said. "I know it seems like a good way to make some cash, but these people... they ain' good people, Randy. I don' wan ta see you mixed up with them. You hear?"

Randy frowned. "But you do it."

"Yeah, I just... I don' gut dreams like you do."

He still didn't understand, but he knew it wouldn't do any good to argue. "Okay. I won' do it again."

"Good man. Now go an' get some sleep." Rene drove off before Randy could even wish him goodnight.

Randy went inside. He made his mozzarella sticks, skirting both the hole in the kitchen floor that opened to the cellar beneath, and the spots in the floor that were fixing to become holes but hadn't broken through yet. He went into the living room and sat down on a couch that was probably more mold than fabric at this point. He grabbed a bag of weed and his pipe off the coffee table and got a little high, then went to play his game... but stopped. Maybe this was what Jessica was talking about. Here he was, almost four in the morning, almost time to wake up and go to work, and he was getting high and playing video games. And he'd had a strange night, a night that, the more he thought about it, was a little sketchy. Maybe even illegal. Rene was right, he shouldn't do it again. And from here on out, he should try to get some rest at night. And maybe lay off the weed. He was going to change.

But he was already high tonight, and there was no point in going to bed this close to morning anyway. He took another hit and started up his game. He was going to change. Tomorrow.

About the Authors

Thomas Benz won the 2017 Serena McDonald Kennedy Award for a short story collection ("Home &Castle") sponsored by Snake Nation Press. He has had nineteen stories published with magazines such as *The Madison Review, William and Mary Review, Mud Season Review*, and others. He was twice a finalist in the Flannery O'Connor Short Fiction Collection Contest. He won the Solstice Short Fiction Contest in 2011 and again in 2018, and was awarded third place in the 2020 Hypertext Review fiction contest. His website is https://indielit.net. His Facebook page is www.facebook.com/ThomasBenzWriter.

Andrew Carlo is a husband, father and forester who lives in Huntington, Vermont. He writes mostly about his parents but sometimes about other things that seem important. He likes sugaring and cutting firewood. His heroes are his parents (Joyce and Don Carlo), Henry Knox, Frederick Law Olmstead and Leon Russell.

Mary D. Chaffee's fascination with dark tales began at an early age, when she and her brothers scared themselves silly with readings from that master of purple-prosed horror fiction, H. P. Lovecraft. *The Return*, included in this anthology, grew out of a prompt in author Nancy Kilgore's long-running BWW workshop: Writing with Spirit. Or perhaps we should think of it as Writing with...*spirits*...

Originally from Massachusetts, **Isabelle Edgar** is currently a student at Stanford University studying English.

Often employing myth, art, and nature, **Malisa Garlieb** writes personal histories while simultaneously unfolding archetypes. She is Poetry Editor for *Mud Season Review*. Her poems have appeared in *Painted Bride Quarterly, Calyx, Tar River Poetry, RHINO Poetry, Rust + Moth, Blue Unicorn, Fourteen Hills, Sugar House Review*, and elsewhere. *Handing Out Apples in Eden* is her first poetry collection, and there's a second manuscript in the works. She's also a teacher, energy healer, and artist. Find her at malisagarlieb.com.

Amy K. Genova lives in Washington state. She received her M.A. in English with an emphasis on writing from Ball State University. A reader for *Mud Season Review*, she published a book of poems entitled, *Flavor Box*. Her poems appear in *3Elements, Cream City Review, Ghost City Press, The R.E.A.L., Flying Island, Homestead Review,* and others. Her ekphrastic poems show in galleries beside representative artwork; "A Life in Yellow--Redux," was chosen for a juried show. Her memoir, *Moving*, was published in *Stonecrop*.

Masha Harris is a native Vermonter who loves telling stories about the characters she knew growing up on the Canadian border. She is forever striving to capture their accents. Her work has appeared in *Potash Hill* and *Chrysalis: The Journal of Transformative Language Arts*.

Olga J. Hebert is a retired Vermont educator who has time to spend with grandchildren, travel, paint, and write poetry. She spends her time between Williston, Vt. and Venice, Fla., always seeking new ways to learn and improve her artistic efforts. She is a member of Venice Poets, Writing Within, Blue Lotus Meditation Center, and the UU Congregation of Venice, all of which provide numerous and satisfying volunteer opportunities.

Mark Hoffman grew up in Minnesota and attended Lawrence University in Wisconsin. After college he moved to New York City and lived there for 20 years, taking time out for graduate school. Mark and his son moved to Vermont in 2008, enjoying the state's unique qualities for life and work.

Leanne Hoppe holds an MFA in poetry from Boston University. She works as a writer and educator in Central Vermont. Her work has been published most recently in *High Shelf Press,* Poetry Online, *This is Not Where I Belong,* and *Palooka Magazine.*

John Kaufmann is a former lawyer and current mobile home park owner who lives in southern New York State. His writing has been published in *Off Assignment, The High Plains Register, Litro, The Journal of the Taxation of Financial Products, The Journal of Taxation of Investments,* and *Tax Notes.*

Karen Kish taught high school English for 25 years in Essex Junction, Vt. She and her husband Sandy also spent 15 years teaching high school in Poland, Egypt, and Hungary. Currently retired, she now enjoys cross-country skiing, traveling, biking, tennis, gardening (especially blueberries and raspberries!), and fun time with family, and is writing a memoir about her and her husband's international teaching adventures.

Katherine Lazarus is a writer from Vermont. She received a MFA in poetry from Bennington College and attended the New England Young Writers Conference at Bread Loaf. She has read for Flour City Readings and her work appears in *Bloodroot Literary Magazine, The Decadent Review,* and *Meow Meow Pow Pow Literary Magazine.* She has worked as a journalist, editor, and copywriter and skis, hikes, and runs in her free time.

Janet McKeehan-Medina grew up in Los Angeles and currently lives in New York with her husband. She is a trained psychotherapist and special education consultant. She has always harbored a passion for writing. As a Burlington Writers Workshop member and volunteer, she was able to reconnect with her love for poetry. During the pandemic, she kept herself centered through the practice of Wild Writing. It allowed her space to process and heal. She will start running groups this summer as a certified Wild Writing teacher. You may find her at janetmckeehanmedina@gmail.com or her website www.janetmckeehanmedina.com.

Phoebe Paron feels lucky to have lived in Burlington, Vt. for 6 years now. It was her childhood dream to be a poet; now she writes for fun. She is an adaptive ski and snowboard instructor in the winter and a gardener in the growing season. She loves the natural world and always has a lovely time observing all that goes on in it.

Charles Lewis Radke's memoir, *Stuccoville: Life Without a Net* (WiDo, Salt Lake City, Utah), came out in January 2021. His creative nonfiction has appeared in *Stoneboat Literary Journal, Sierra Nevada Review, Palante, Showbear Family Circus, HASH,* and others. His short fiction has appeared in *Mud Season Review, The San Joaquin Review, Hayden's Ferry Review, Gulf Stream Magazine,* and *The South Dakota Review.* He is the recipient of an AWP Intro Award for fiction and the Estelle Campbell Prize for literature from the National Society of Arts and Letters.

Erin Ruble's essays and short fiction have appeared in *Boulevard, Green Mountains Review, Tahoma Literary Review,* and elsewhere. Originally from Montana, she now lives in Vermont with her husband and children. You can find her at erinruble.wordpress.com.

Alicia Tebeau-Sherry is a recent graduate of the University of Vermont; she graduated with a major in English and a minor in Nutrition, and now works in communications for the Town of Colchester. While studying at the University of Vermont, she was co-editor-in-chief of the university's literary and visual arts journal, *The Gist*, in which many of her poems were published. She also shared her love for writing with her peers by tutoring for the University of Vermont's Undergraduate Writing Center. When not writing poetry or enjoying a good book, you can find her running, baking banana bread, or singing along to her favorite musicians.

Christopher "Kit" Storjohann is a writer, photographer, and meditation teacher who lives in Barre, Vt. Kit's work has appeared in the anthologies *Seven Voices: Volume One* (2015) and *Seven Voices: Volume Two* (2018), both published by The New Atlantean Library, and *Beach Reads: Paradise* (2019) published by Third Street Writers, Inc., as well as in numerous publications including *Bluing the Blade*, *The Moving Force Journal*, *Toho Journal*, *Kosmos Journal*, *Prometheus Dreaming* and *The Hummingbird Post*, which named Kit their Best Emerging Writer of 2019.

Libby Conrad VanBuskirk lives in Shelburne, Vt. and has published poetry in the *Beloit Poetry Journal*, *Blueline*, *the Aurorean*, in anthologies, and elsewhere. She won a grant award from the Society of Children's Book Writers and Illustrators and authored *Beyond the Stones of Machu Picchu*, a book of short stories. Early in her career, she was awarded an interview with T.S. Eliot. A member of the Vermont Otter Creek Poets, over the past year she has studied poetry with Rebecca Starks. Her other specialty relates to Inca art and history, which she studied at The Radcliffe Institute and co-taught courses at the University of Vermont.

Candelin Wahl is a dog lover who carries treats in her pockets, but doesn't have any pets, except a hedgehog puppet named "Henny" and two sweet grand-dogs. Through poetry and songwriting, she explores relationships in all their messiness. She's a cyclist, hiker and devoted new grandmother who lives and writes in Burlington, Vt. Please find her at https://www.candelinwahl.com/; on Twitter and IG @beachdreamvt.

Acknowledgements

The Burlington Writers Workshop acknowledges our dynamic writing community for their enthusiasm, creativity, and commitment to the art of writing. We extend appreciation to our workshop leaders for offering high-quality workshops, encouraging the creative process, and providing invaluable guidance and feedback. We thank our volunteers for their dedicated hours of service in providing all that Burlington Writers Workshop has to offer. Special thanks to Susan Smereka for our cover art, and to all of the writers who have contributed to this year's anthology.